For:
BOS – welcome to the Family!

OBE (Order of the Bloody Entrails) to:
Becky Peacock – for braving warehouse hell.
Every. Single. Time.

My Family of editors:
Venetia Gosling
Elv Moody
Kate Sullivan

Christopher Little Agency – we are Family!

ZOM-B

ZOM-B FAMILY

DARREN SHAN

SIMON AND SCHUSTER

First published in Great Britain in 2014 by Simon and Schuster UK Ltd
A CBS COMPANY

1 3 5 7 9 10 8 6 4 2

Simon & Schuster UK Ltd
1st Floor
222 Gray's Inn Road
London WC1X 8HB

www.simonandschuster.co.uk

Simon & Schuster Australia, Sydney
Simon & Schuster India, New Delhi

A CIP catalogue record for this book
is available from the British Library.

HB ISBN: 978-0-85707-784-4
TPB ISBN: 978-0-85707-785-1
EBOOK ISBN: 978-0-85707-787-5

Printed and bound by CPI Group (UK) Ltd, Croydon, CR0 4YY

THEN . . .

Becky Smith's father was a bullying racist. For the sake of a quiet life, she never challenged him. But when he made her sacrifice a black boy at her school to a pack of zombies, she finally rebelled and severed the ties between them.

B was turned into a zombie shortly after fleeing from her father. Several months later she recovered her senses in an underground facility, where she was held prisoner with the zom heads, a pack of conscious zombies. A soldier called Josh Massoglia was in command until the complex was invaded by a crazy clown and his army of mutants. The psychotic Mr Dowling set B free, then went on his merry way.

After another run-in with the clown on the streets of London, in which he again saved her life, B joined the Angels, a group of revitalised teenagers working under the guidance of the century-old Dr Oystein to defeat Mr Dowling and restore order to the world. After an uncomfortable period of adjustment, she started to get along with the Angels, except for Rage, a cynical hulk with selfish, murderous tendencies. She could never bring herself to trust Rage, but tolerated him because Dr Oystein saw promise in the brute.

Dr Oystein wasn't the only person trying to restore control. The members of the Board – a collection of billionaires and politicians – were trying to establish a new order in which they could rule over the living survivors. B got on the wrong side of one of them, the despicable Dan-Dan, a giggling, child-killing monster. He was in league with the mysterious Owl Man, an ex-associate of Dr Oystein's, and the pair were backed by a menacing offshoot of the Ku Klux Klan.

B and Rage captured Dan-Dan, but Owl Man was holding B's best friend, Vinyl, hostage, along with a group of prisoners from a town called New Kirkham. They agreed to swap Dan-Dan for Vinyl and, if possible, the other hostages, and Rage set off on Dr Oystein's orders to Battersea Power Station, where the Klanners were based. Two other Angels went with him, but B was told to remain in County Hall, since Owl Man was able to control her mind and might turn her against her comrades.

B disobeyed that command and trailed the others to the Power Station. There, as the swap was about to be made, Rage slaughtered the unsuspecting pair of Angels and betrayed B. A delighted Dan-Dan told his troops to open fire and finish her off. That should have been the end of B Smith, but then an unexpected figure burst from the ranks of the hood-wearing KKK and demanded mercy. To B's amazement, it was her father, alive and well and as racist as ever, coming to her rescue.

NOW . . .

ONE

The guy who handcuffs me is wearing gloves so thick that you could safely handle radioactive material with them. Even so, he sweats buckets until the cuffs snap shut and he's able to withdraw. He knows I'm undead and one tiny scratch from me is all it would take to end his life.

Meek as a lamb, I let myself be led inside the converted Power Station. I'm in total shock. I've thought about Dad and Mum often since I recovered my senses, wondered what happened to them, if they got out of London, if they were alive or dead. For Mum's sake, I'd hoped they'd made it to a compound or one of the zombie-free islands. But secretly I thought they were both goners.

Now Dad has popped up out of nowhere, in the middle of my enemies, to save me from what would have otherwise been certain death. I don't know how to react, whether to feel grateful or hateful.

Things were always weird between us. I loved him so much. He was clever and funny, thoughtful and protective, in some ways a perfect father. He provided for me and Mum, fought for us when he had to, gave us all that he could. When he heard about the zombies, his first instinct was to rescue me. He risked his life for mine.

At the same time he was a racist bully. He beat Mum and me regularly, usually for no good reason. He told me to hate anyone of a different colour or creed. He tried to turn me into a mirror image of him, a creature of bigotry and loathing.

I didn't want to grow up like my dad, but I never stood up to him. I chuckled at his insulting jokes. I read the hate lit that he stacked our bookshelves with.

I pretended to share his twisted beliefs. Over time, the act became reality and, to my shame and horror, I began behaving like him. I think, given a few more years, I might have turned into a daughter he could have been truly proud of.

Vinyl used to warn me about the dangers of putting on an act. He was my best mate, but we had to keep our friendship secret or my dad would have hit the roof. Vinyl often urged me to take a stand. But I couldn't. I was too afraid.

I look around for the first time as I'm hustled through a series of rooms in the massive building. Most are loaded with supplies — food, drink, weapons. No beds. I guess the sleeping quarters are located on the upper levels.

All of the external windows are bricked up. Through the internal windows I can see into a courtyard. Glimpses of cages and hundreds of blacks, Arabs and Asians huddled together miserably, soldiers and hooded Klanners keeping watch over their prisoners.

My dad's marching beside me. He looks at me

every so often and smiles. His fingers twitch and I know he wants to reach out and hug me, or at least stroke my hair. But then he clocks the hole in my chest where my heart should be, green moss growing thickly around it, and he reminds himself that he can never touch me again.

Dan-Dan is on my other side. He's beaming like a child at Christmas. He keeps shaking his head and giggling. He wanted to bring me in, torture me, experiment on me and treat me to a long, slow, drawn-out death. Owl Man wouldn't play ball. When I begged him to let me die with dignity rather than be taken into custody, he insisted on a swift execution.

Dad's unexpected appearance changed all that. I surrendered instead of fighting to the death. I think Owl Man saw that as a chance to save me. For some bizarre reason, he doesn't want me dead. But Dan-Dan does and, as far as that filthy child-killer is concerned, he has me where he wants me, under his wing, at his mercy, ripe for the plucking.

I can't see Owl Man, but I can hear the clatter of

his dog's paws on the floor behind me, so I'm guessing he's back there with Sakarias, his mutant hound. I'm betting Rage is with him, but I don't want to think about that back-stabbing bastard, so I deliberately tune him out of my thoughts.

We enter the courtyard and I squint against the sunlight — if there was a roof over this place before, it's been removed, leaving the yard open to the elements. I left my hat and glasses outside. I didn't think I'd need them any more when I took them off. Now I wish I'd paused to pick them up. The light is blinding for a zombie like me.

'Are you uncomfortable, poor little dead girl?' Dan-Dan simpers. 'Would you like me to fetch a hat for you, or call Coley and borrow a pair of his oh-so-trendy shades?'

'All I want you to do, fat man,' I growl, 'is stick your head up your arse and eat yourself from the inside out.'

'What a delightfully horrible thing to say,' Dan-Dan cries, clapping his hands in admiration. 'You raised a real beast, Tom.'

'Todd,' Dad corrects him quietly. He winces at having to speak back. He was always subdued around powerful people.

I was expecting a stench from the cages, but the air is thick with the smell of disinfectant. I spot teams of cleaners scrubbing down the ground around the prisoners. Then I remember that humans can't afford to leave a mess. Waste attracts flies and other insects, which can spread the zombie gene.

The people in the cages don't pay much attention to me, but the soldiers and Klanners are fascinated. They follow my every footstep. Some call out insults, but most just watch warily.

I'm led across the courtyard and into the structure on the opposite side. I glance up at the famous chimneys before I pass into the gloom. They're an impressive sight. I wonder if this is the last time I'll ever see them.

Then we're marching through another series of rooms. The walls here have been reinforced with metal sheets bolted into place. The doors are thick steel. We stop at one which is locked and a soldier hurries to open it. He steps out of the way and nods for me to enter.

'Wait a minute,' somebody calls out before I step in, and a figure from my past comes strolling towards me.

'Josh Massoglia,' I sneer. 'Why am I not surprised?'

Josh is smiling. The soldier looks as handsome and well-groomed as he did back in the underground complex, where he was the boss along with a scientist called Dr Cerveris. His charms were always lost on me – I never had much time for pretty boys – but Cathy, a fellow zom head, used to go weak at the knees whenever he walked into a room, and I think most girls would be the same.

'It's been a long time, Becky,' he greets me.

'Not long enough,' I grunt.

'As charming as ever,' he grins, coming to a stop a metre from me. He's dressed in his army uniform and is clean-shaven, reeking of what was no doubt an expensive cologne back when money meant something. He looks over my head and his face darkens. I guess he's spotted Rage.

'No need to say anything,' Rage says brightly. 'I can tell you're overwhelmed to see me again.'

'That was a strange scene outside,' Josh murmurs distastefully. 'It takes a special breed of person to turn on his own without even a flicker of guilt.'

'What can I say?' Rage laughs. 'I was born blessed.'

Josh's eyes are hard, but he leaves it there and returns his attention to me. He studies my wrists, cuffed behind my back. 'I can have those removed if you promise to behave.'

'Like hell you will,' Dan-Dan barks. 'She'd go for us in the blink of an eye.'

'Not me,' I say sweetly. 'I'm a good girl, I am.' Then I gnash my teeth at Josh and make a growling noise.

Josh shrugs. 'Have it your way. I just wanted to help.'

'You don't have to do anything for me,' I tell him, stepping into the room and facing the door, waiting for it to slam shut. 'I don't need creature comforts. Just a coffin when Dan-Dan's done with me.'

'Oh, I don't think that will be necessary,' Dan-Dan purrs as the door starts to swing closed. 'There won't be enough left to warrant a coffin by the time I'm finished.' He blows me a kiss. 'Sweet dreams, my darling.'

TWO

Dan-Dan's parting shot is ironical. He knows I can't sleep. The undead are denied that simple pleasure.

The room is small, no more than three metres by three. There's a metal bench bolted firmly to one wall, but that's it as far as luxuries go. Steel plates cover the walls and ceiling, fixed tightly into place. Dim, artificial light seeps through a series of cracks in the plates overhead.

I stand by the door for ages, thinking about what has happened, marvelling at the fact that Dad is alive, wondering if Mum is with him. I also ask myself if it's pure coincidence that he was here in Battersea, waiting for me. Owl Man knew who he was before he removed his hood. Has the creep with the large eyes been pulling strings, or did he just recognise my father's voice?

When no one comes to interrogate me, I sit on the bench and stare off into space. I can't see any CCTV cameras, but I'm sure I'm being filmed. I'd flick the voyeurs the finger if I could, but my hands are bound securely behind my back.

A cold ball of fire burns in my stomach as I remember what Rage did to Pearse and Conall. I warned everyone not to trust him. He's a sly, savage, self-serving creep. He almost had me fooled. I'd started to doubt my instincts, to accept him as a well-meaning Angel.

The most frustrating part is that Rage was honest with me. He told me he was looking for action and adventure. He stuck with us as long as he did because he had nothing better to do with his time. When Dan-Dan came along with offers of power and life on a paradise island ... Well, leopards don't change their spots.

I should have *known*. I feel responsible for what happened to Conall and Pearse. I could have rammed an ice pick through Rage's head long ago. I let Dr Oystein talk me out of tackling him. I should have listened to my gut, taken my punishment if the doc had condemned me. Too bloody nice, that's my problem!

Time drags. I'm used to that – life's a bitch when you can't sleep – but it's harder when I can't see the sun or moon. No way to judge if it's day or night, or how long I've been here. The last time I was this removed from the daily routines of the outside world was in the underground complex.

Later, as I'm still brooding about Rage, the door opens and Dad enters. I spot soldiers in the corridor, armed with rifles and flame-throwers. Josh is behind my father. 'You're sure you want to do this?' he asks.

Dad nods. 'She's my daughter. She won't hurt me.'

'You've more faith in her than I have,' Josh grunts, but steps aside and lets a guard bring a chair into the room. The soldiers exit and close the door. Dad sits down across from me.

'How are you doing?'

'Better than you,' I mutter. He looks about thirty years older than when I last saw him. Hair streaked with grey. Face lined with wrinkles. There's a tremor in his hands which he can't control.

'I guess I'm a sight,' he says wearily. 'It hasn't been easy. The undead are better off in lots of ways. There have been plenty of times when I wished I hadn't made it out alive.'

'Me too,' I grin viciously.

Dad cocks his head, not sure if I'm joking or serious.

'*Mum?*' I whisper.

Dad pretends he hasn't heard. Instead he pulls out a hand grenade from a pocket and plays with it. 'I carry this with me wherever I go,' he says, staring transfixed at the grenade as if it's a holy relic. 'I took it from a corpse a long time ago, the day London fell.

Or maybe it was a few days later. I'm not sure. My brain goes a bit wonky whenever I think back that far.

'This is how I want to go when my time comes,' he continues, tugging gently at the pin, enough to disturb it slightly but not pull it out. 'When those brain-munching bastards finally catch up, I'll set this off and take a few of them to Hell with me. Quick and messy, that's the way to sign off. I don't want to become a walking abomination like . . .' He pauses.

'. . . me?' I finish.

'Yeah.' Dad smiles sadly and puts the grenade away. 'You hurt me, Becky. You shouldn't have run away. I loved you and risked everything for you. When you turned your back on me, it was like you'd stabbed me through the heart.'

'You made me kill Tyler,' I retort stiffly.

'He didn't matter,' Dad says.

'Because he was black?' I sneer.

'Yeah.' Dad's eyes never leave mine. 'Life's a battle. It's what I tried to teach you since you were born. We all belong to a side. You have to stick with your own and make sure your enemies never gain enough power to drive you under. You think your black friend wouldn't have thrown you to the monsters if the shoe had been on the other foot?'

'You're sick,' I snarl. 'With all that's happened, you're lost in the past, a relic of a time that doesn't exist any more.'

'Oh, it exists,' Dad says. 'Nothing has changed fundamentally. It's still us against them.'

'What about the zombies?' I challenge him.

'They're irrelevant,' he says and I gawp at him with astonishment.

'How the hell can you say that?' I cry.

'Because it's true,' he replies. 'They're dangerous, yeah, a threat that we have to eliminate. But they're not a thinking, scheming menace. We'll get rid of them eventually, wipe the planet clean of their stain. But the blacks will still be here. The Muslims and their Taliban pit bulls. The Chinese and Russians and Indians, empire-builders with their dreams of ruling the roost and crushing the rest of us under their heels.

'The zombies are an opportunity,' Dad says.

'Society has been reset. The first nation out of the blocks will have an advantage over the others. This is a time to cull, to set out our stall and make this country great again. We'll deal with our problems, come through the war with the undead pure and united, then take on the rest of the world and turn it into a place we can be proud of.'

'You're crazy,' I jeer. 'Mankind has been reduced to its bare bones. The living are an endangered species. Race and religion should mean less now than they ever did. You all need to band together if you're going to recover.'

He shakes his head. 'We don't see it that way. We see this as a blessing, a time for the strong and pure to stand up and be counted. This is our chance to rid ourselves of those who've been dragging us down, who hate us just as much as we hate them, who would wipe us out if they ever got the chance.'

I stare at him helplessly. 'But you need them. When I was trying to get out of my school, I needed the help of other kids, black, Asian, whatever.'

'That's where you're wrong,' he says. 'If you'd

thrown those kids to the zombies, you would have had a better chance of getting out. The zombies would have lost interest in you if you'd given them others to rip apart and eat.'

'So, what, you plan to sacrifice everyone who isn't white? Let the zombies eat them all?'

'Yeah,' he says calmly.

'You're crazy,' I tell him again. 'There won't be enough of you left to win the war with the undead. You'll be destroyed.'

'No,' he says. 'There are enough of us. You've seen our troops here, and there are lots more in other cities and bases around the country. We're a genuine force, growing all the time as more and more survivors – *our* kind of survivors – throw their support behind us. This used to be our world, and it always should have been. We're taking it back.'

'No,' I say. 'What you're doing is turning it into a hellhole.'

'Hell for anyone we don't like,' Dad smirks. 'Heaven for those who are worthy of Heaven.'

'You're scum,' I whisper and look away. It pains me

that this man is my father. I wish I could rid my body of every last gene that he passed on to me.

'Watch your bloody language,' Dad growls. 'I'm your father. I'm due some respect.'

'Not when you behave like this, you don't.'

Dad clenches his hands angrily. Then he sighs and lets them relax. 'I was so hurt when you betrayed me,' he says, returning to what is obviously a sore point. 'All the love and care I showered on you, and that was how you repaid me.'

'What about all the times you hit me?' I snap. 'The times you used Mum and me as punchbags?'

'It's a hard world,' he shrugs. 'I was trying to toughen you up.'

I laugh sickly. 'Well, it worked. Here I am, Dad, an undead killer. I hope you're proud of me.'

'I am actually,' he says. 'Lord Wood told me what you've been through. Most people would have crumbled long ago, given what you've had to deal with. I regret nothing about the way I brought you up. You're a warrior, and a lot of that is down to how I raised you.'

'Yeah, well, be careful what you create. If I treated you coldly, it's your own fault for not teaching me to be more loving.'

'There might be truth in that,' Dad says thoughtfully. 'I always adored you, but maybe I should have been more open about my feelings, told you more often that you meant the world to me, that I was only ever cruel because I wanted to be kind, because I feared losing you if you weren't strong enough to make your own way in the world.'

I shift uneasily on the bench. This is what I always hated most about Dad, the way he could appear reasonable and vulnerable. If he'd been an unfeeling monster all the time, I could have simply loathed him. But right now I feel like *I'm* in the wrong, even though *he's* the racist supremacist.

'How'd you get out?' I ask, trying to steer him on to a different topic.

'It was difficult,' he says, wincing at the memories. 'I fought and killed, ran and struggled. I knew I had to get clear of London quickly. I realised the zombies didn't like the sun. Once night fell, the city would go to hell. I darted home, picked up a few things that I needed, then hit the road on foot.'

'What about Mum?' I ask. 'Was she one of the things you needed?'

Dad glares at me, then again acts as if I hadn't asked about her.

'I made it to the suburbs and holed up before sunset. A lot of people banded together, but I figured that would make them more of a target, so I kept to myself. The screams that first night . . .' He shudders. 'I wanted to creep out and let the bastards kill me, just to escape the screams. I still hear them when I dream. Sometimes when I'm awake too.'

His expression goes distant and there's a short silence. Despite everything, I feel sorry for him and part of me wishes I could have been there with him to help share the pain.

'I kept walking the next day,' he continues. 'I didn't have a plan. It was total chaos. Nobody knew if we could repel the zombies. We thought it might be the end of the world. I spent a few weeks wandering the countryside, keeping to open fields by day, locking myself into small buildings at night.

'Finally I joined one of the settlements that were springing up, a walled town. By sheer luck it was one of the first Klan-friendly towns. Smarter people than me had seen the opportunity immediately and set up a few whites-only towns where we could gather, recruit and grow strong.'

'Sounds like you had a right jolly time.'

He nods slowly. 'I loved it and I won't pretend otherwise. It was hard, and we went through all kinds of hell, but I saw the seeds of a new society being sown. I came to see the downfall of the old society as something that had to happen. We couldn't have thinned our ranks the way we needed to if not for the zombies. In a weird way, like I said before, they've been a blessing.'

I moan with horror. 'You're unbelievable.'

'Just being honest,' he says. 'I always played my cards straight. You knew where you stood with me from day one.'

'Yeah,' I mutter. 'And I've cursed myself more

31

times than you can imagine for not crawling away from you on day two.'

Dad laughs heartily. 'That's my girl. Always with a quick, cutting comeback. I've missed that about you, B. That and a lot of other things.'

'Well, lap it up while you can,' I say sullenly. 'You won't have me for long.'

'What are you talking about?' he frowns.

'Dan-Dan will make short work of me.'

'Lord Wood?' Dad shakes his head. 'He's given me his word that he'll let you live if you cooperate with us. I know there's been bad blood between the two of you, but if you join us and work to help us grow even stronger than we already are, he'll put that behind him and let you be.'

'Bullshit,' I snort. 'He's a child-killing sicko who has it in for me. My days are numbered, and yours will be too if you get in his way.'

'No,' Dad says. 'You've got him wrong. He'll leave you alone if you treat him with the respect he deserves. This can be a new start for us. We can be a family again, carry on where we left off, make things right.'

'You're off your head,' I huff.

'I'm your father,' he thunders. 'Watch your tongue.'

'Or what?' I throw back at him.

He starts to get to his feet, hand swinging wide to slap me, old habits kicking in. Then he remembers what I am and stops, crestfallen.

'What's wrong, Daddy dearest?' I simper. 'Oh, that's right, you can't beat me up any more, can you? Unless you want to go get a plank to hammer me over the head with.'

'Don't say such things,' he croaks, sitting again, looking on the verge of tears.

'Why not?' I shout. 'You never gave a damn about me really. You only wanted me around so that you could turn me into a mini version of yourself. You want to start over? You care about family? My arse! You don't know what that means. What happened to Mum? You haven't mentioned her. If you're such a big family man, that's the first thing you would have told me. Go on, Dad, let me have it. Did you look for her? Did she even cross your mind?'

'Of course she did,' he yells. 'The flat was the first place I went after you left me in the lurch. I shouldn't have gone back. It made more sense to keep running. But I had to search for her. She was my wife. I loved her.'

'And?' I whisper when he doesn't continue, fearing the worst, sure he's going to tell me he couldn't find her or that she was dead when he got there. Instead he shocks me.

'She's here,' he mumbles.

'What?' I'm not sure I heard him right.

'She's here,' he says again, 'in a room a few corridors further along.'

'Mum's here?' I gasp, leaping to my feet, staring at him with eyes almost as wide as Owl Man's. 'Why didn't you bring her to see me?'

'It's not that simple,' he says, looking away shiftily.

'Why not?' I growl. Dad sighs and doesn't answer. 'Come on, tell me — why not?' I roar.

He looks up at me angrily, then spits on the floor and says petulantly, 'Because she's a bloody zombie.'

THREE

For a long time I'm too numb to say anything. When I can speak again, I tell Dad I want to see her. He says he doesn't think that's a good idea. I tell him I don't care what he thinks, that if he doesn't take me to her, I won't say another word. I'll just sit here in silence until they starve me or kill me. When he realises I'm serious, he says he'll ask for permission, but he can't promise anything.

I sit in a cold rage when Dad leaves, head whirring. I'm not sure how to react. My chat with Dad has left me bewildered. Part of me is glad he's alive, but another part wishes he had died rather than joined the KKK.

He's a hate-mongering, nasty piece of work, there's no getting away from that. But he's still my father. He risked his life (again) to save me today. He's eager to reconnect. He wants the best for me. How can I truly hate someone who loves me so much?

I get to my feet and march round the room, one lap after another, trying to distract myself by keeping active. I'm sorry now that I didn't agree to let them free my hands. My arms feel like dead weights behind my back.

Finally the door opens again. But it's not Dad who steps in this time. It's Dan-Dan. His loyal crony Coley is with him. The grinning guard in the stylish sunglasses nods at me in a friendly manner then trains a taser on me.

'If you move, I'll fry you,' Coley says.

'Yeah, yeah,' I yawn, focusing on the organ-grinder rather than the monkey.

'Have you missed me, little one?' Dan-Dan smirks.

'Like crazy,' I sneer. 'Come over here, nice and close, so I can kiss you.'

'I think not,' he chuckles, then raises an eyebrow. 'I hear you'd like to see your mother.' I glower at him silently. 'Well?' he sings when I don't respond. 'Do you want to see her or not?'

'Yeah,' I mumble.

'I'm the one who decides whether she can have visitors,' he says.

'So don't let me see her,' I sniff. 'Like I give a damn.'

'Oh, but I think you do,' he says. 'What caring daughter wouldn't? I'm not a heartless beast, Becky. I don't want to stand in the way of a touching reunion. But you'll have to do something for me first.'

'What?' I snap.

Dan-Dan smiles beatifically. 'Ask politely.'

I scowl at him. 'That's all? You don't want me to kill someone or dance on hot coals or tell you all my secrets?'

'Of course not. I simply want you to ask nicely, like a good girl.'

I don't want to give him the satisfaction. I want to tell him to get stuffed. But I'll gain nothing if I do that. This is one of those rare occasions where I have to bite my tongue and be diplomatic. That doesn't come naturally to me, but I can do it when I need to. I think.

'Please let me see my mum,' I growl, the words like nails in my throat.

Dan-Dan glances at Coley. 'What do you think?'

'Pathetic,' Coley jeers.

'I agree.' Dan-Dan looks at me again. 'You can be sweeter than that, I'm sure.'

I mutter something foul under my breath, then force a sickly smile. 'Please let me go and see my mother.'

'That sounded almost human,' he laughs. 'But try it again, with more feeling.'

'Please –'

'Lord Wood,' he murmurs.

'Please, Lord Wood,' I say through gritted teeth, 'I'd like to visit my mother. Will you let me?'

'Good,' he nods. 'I could make you beg, but that's

38

enough for now. Of course you can visit her. I'll lead you to her straight away. See? I can be the most helpful man in the world if you cooperate with me.'

'Thank you,' I croak.

Dan-Dan steps out into the corridor and I follow, Coley just behind me, prodding me with the tip of the taser. Dan-Dan guides me through a couple of similar corridors, then we come to a door much like the one to my room. Dad is standing outside. He smiles when he sees me.

'I told you she'd respond positively,' he says.

'You did indeed, Todd,' Dan-Dan booms. 'I stand corrected, and I'm glad to be wrong in this instance. Open the door and let us pass.'

There's a key in the lock. Dad turns it and pushes the door open. Dan-Dan enters the room, makes me wait a moment, then beckons me in. Dad comes too. And Coley, of course.

There's a steel bed in the middle of the room. Mum is lying spread-eagled on it. Her feet and hands are chained, holding her in place like a pinned insect. She's naked. There's a sheet lying on the floor to her left. Dan-Dan tuts, picks it up and covers her with it. 'Sorry you had to see that,' he whispers, but by the glint in his eyes I'm sure he's secretly ecstatic. He might even have come in here in advance and yanked it off her.

I stare at my mother with horror. She's in good condition. They must keep her fed. Her eyes are brighter than most reviveds' and her hair hasn't lost too much of its sheen. There are moss-encrusted scratches down her right arm, and I saw more across her thighs before Dan-Dan covered them. But the bones sticking out of her fingers and toes have been filed down, as have the fangs in her mouth.

'Mum?' I moan, stepping forward into view, hoping against hope that she'll recognise me and react.

The zombie stares at me, clocking me as one of her own, but only of her own species. She loses interest when she realises my brain is of no use to her. Instead she focuses on the humans and snarls, straining against the chains, trying to break free.

'When was she last fed?' Dan-Dan asks.

'A few days ago,' Dad says quietly.

'Shall we top her up?' he beams.

'I don't think we need to right now,' Dad says miserably.

'It would be cruel not to,' Dan-Dan says. 'She's hungry, poor thing. We must treat our guests with all the kindness that we can.'

Dan-Dan nods at Coley. He passes the taser to Dan-Dan before fetching a bucket from a corner of the room. I catch the scent of fresh brains. Dan-Dan must have had them delivered ahead of our meeting. Coley pulls on heavy-duty gloves and a mask, then picks up a scrap of brain. He leans over my mother's face and drops the sliver of brain into her mouth, like a bird feeding its chick. She makes a mewling sound and swallows eagerly. Coley drops in more of the grey chunks and she chews mechanically, her features relaxing. She doesn't struggle to break free any more. When she's had enough, Coley steps back and returns the bucket to its corner. He doesn't remove the gloves or mask.

'How long must we wait?' Dan-Dan asks.

'Less than a minute,' Coley says.

A few seconds later Mum vomits over herself. Most zombies need to stick a finger down their throat to do that. Lacking the use of her hands, Mum must have developed a slicker method of ridding her stomach of waste matter. She goes on vomiting until it's all been forced up. Then she lies back, smiling softly, sated, covered in her own puke.

Coley hauls across another bucket, this one filled with water. He gets a brush and scrubs her down. The sheet is speckled with vomit. He removes it, balls it up and leaves her lying there, naked again.

'Have you no other sheet to cover her with?' Dan-Dan asks, feigning surprise.

'Not at the moment, my Lord,' Coley says, removing his mask and pushing up his sunglasses to wink at me.

'What a pity,' Dan-Dan sighs. He strolls round the bed, studying her. 'She was a good-looking woman, wasn't she?'

I don't say anything. Neither does Dad. He's staring at the floor, cheeks red, torn between shame and

43

anger. He knows Dan-Dan is using Mum to hurt me. He doesn't like it. But there's nothing he can do. He's chosen his masters, so he has to bend to their whims.

'How did she end up here?' I ask Dad.

'She'd been turned when I got to the flat,' he says. 'She'd eaten the brain of one of our neighbours, so she was docile. I tied her up before I left. I figured, if I didn't, she'd wander off and I'd never be able to find her.'

'Why didn't you just bash her bloody head open and finish her off?'

He stares at me. 'She's my wife.'

'Was,' I correct him. 'She's a zombie now.'

'So are you,' he notes. 'We might be able to cure her, the way you were cured.'

'Impossible,' I snap. 'I revitalised because of the vaccine I was given when I was a child. You can't give her that now — it wouldn't do anything for her.'

'I know,' he says. 'It's been explained to me. But they might develop another vaccine, one that can restore the thought processes of those who've been infected.'

'No way,' I snort. 'There's no hope for a revived like her. It's cruel, keeping her enslaved like this, where the likes of these disgusting creeps can perv over her.'

'*Moi?*' Dan-Dan squeals, feigning shock.

'I don't see it that way,' Dad says. 'I returned to the flat when I came back to London. I told my superiors about her and they helped me transport her here.'

'Owl Man's work,' Dan-Dan says. 'I didn't know about her or your father. He kept them a secret from me.'

'Then he knew that you were here?' I ask Dad.

He nods. 'We didn't talk much. He's a busy man. But he'd seen me around and he was the one who approved Daisy's transfer.'

Daisy. I'd almost forgotten Mum's name.

'I'd like to stay here with her,' I tell them.

'No,' Dan-Dan says.

'Why not?' Dad frowns. 'They'd be company for each other. Maybe Daisy will start recollecting things if they spend more time together.'

Dan-Dan cocks his head. 'Are you challenging me, Todd?'

Dad flushes. 'No, my Lord, of course not. I was just expressing an opinion. I'm sorry if I offended you.'

'You didn't,' Dan-Dan smiles. 'But, in answer to your question, we can't leave your daughter here because I fear she would attack your wife. I'm right, aren't I, Becky? You'd chew through to her brain, to set her shackled soul free, wouldn't you?'

I don't reply, but they can tell from my expression that Dan-Dan hit the nail smack on the head.

Dad's face darkens. 'You should be ashamed of yourself,' he growls.

'I'm ashamed of *you*,' I hit back. 'How can you let them degrade her like this? Do the right thing and execute her. Don't rob her of any more of her dignity.'

'We might be able to help her,' he insists.

'No,' I tell him. 'You can't even help yourself. You're a sad, pitiful creature, and you've dragged her down to your lousy level.'

Dad gawps at me, confused and hurt.

Dan-Dan laughs lightly. 'Such a way with words. You should have been a politician like our friend, Vicky Wedge. Speaking of whom, come, my darling, you have so many people to catch up with. It's time for a tour. Isn't that exciting? I love showing newcomers around. It's such a pleasure to . . .'

I tune out Dan-Dan's prattle as he leads me from the room, focusing instead on my undead mother as the door closes on her, feeling more wretched than I have in a long time, wishing I could help, but knowing I'm in no better a position than she is. In fact I'm worse off. She can't sink any lower than she has. But under Dan-Dan's twisted guardianship, I probably have quite a way yet to fall.

FOUR

I'm taken back to the courtyard, then up one flight
of stairs after another to the very top of the building.
I've got an amazing view of the Power Station from
here, the four chimneys linked by tall walls, shorter
buildings attached to the east and west sides.

Soldiers and Klanners are ranged across the top
of the walls, covering every possible approach.
Nobody's ever going to spring a surprise assault on
these guys.

I'm led to a room in the middle of the north section, between the two chimneys that overlook the

Thames. Long windows make the most of the view. The furniture is of the highest standard, leather chairs, a fancy glass and steel table, digital maps of the world spread across the walls.

Four people are seated at the table. An elderly, white-haired, thick-limbed man, a sharp-faced woman in a smart jacket and trousers, Josh Massoglia in his army fatigues and the pot-bellied Owl Man in his customary suit, Sakarias resting by his feet, happily chewing on a metal bone. I guess the mutant dog would crush real bones as soon as it set its fangs around them.

'We meet again, Miss Smith,' the white-haired man says.

I grin tightly. 'Mr Bazini. The displeasure is all mine.'

Justin Bazini was a multibillionaire and is still very powerful, even though money shouldn't mean anything now. There was no official head of the Board as far as I could tell, but all of the other members bowed to Bazini's authority, even the usually arrogant Dan-Dan.

'The little brat is mocking you, Justin,' the woman says. 'Reprimand her. She has to learn her place.'

'I know my place, Vicky,' I sniff. 'Where's yours?'

'Impudent girl,' she snarls.

Vicky Wedge used to be an ultra-conservative politician, wary of anyone who couldn't trace their British heritage back at least ten generations. I always thought she seemed out of place on HMS *Belfast*. She didn't fit in with the other members of the Board. I wondered why they chose to include her. Now I've sussed it. She must have had ties to the Klan. She was the Board's link to the hood-wearing scum.

Justin and his cronies want to rule the world. I suppose they'll need an army to back them if they're to succeed. Josh's presence is evidence that they have a close relationship with the regular military, but I guess they figured they could do with as many supporters as they could rustle up.

Dan-Dan takes his seat and sticks his feet on the table. He's changed into a policeman's outfit, but is wearing a pair of pink slippers. 'So nice to slip back into these,' he says, noting my surprised look. 'I have such tender feet.'

'This must be Todd,' Justin says, smiling at my dad. 'Please, sit down, make yourself comfortable.'

Dad nods stiffly and sits where directed. He looks like a naughty boy who has been called into the headmaster's office.

Nobody says anything to Coley. He's beneath their interest, but that doesn't seem to bother him. He's happy to stand behind me with his taser, all but invisible, ready to zap me if I make a threatening move.

There's a long silence while the members of the Board study me. I return their stares with disinterest, then glance over their heads at the window behind them, wondering if I could survive a fall from this height.

'Push the thought from your head, Miss Smith,' Justin chuckles humourlessly. 'The window is tempered glass. You would bounce off it like a rubber ball.'

'We don't take chances,' Vicky says. 'Especially after what happened on the *Belfast*.'

'That was a kick in the teeth, wasn't it?' someone chortles. I look round and spot Rage standing in a corner. I should have noticed him when I came in, but I was too focused on the others.

'I'm still angry about that,' Vicky pouts. 'I loved living on the *Belfast*.'

Rage shrugs, strolls over to the table and takes a seat, ignoring Justin's frown. 'I was Dr Oystein's man then. I didn't know about you guys or that I could strike a deal with you. That's changed. I'm on your team now. It'd be silly to bear a grudge.'

'But can we trust him?' Vicky asks Dan-Dan. 'What if he's a spy?'

'He's a damn cold-hearted one if he is,' Dan-Dan laughs. 'He killed the two Angels who came here with him.'

'Dr Oystein accepts the need for losses,' Owl Man says softly. 'He has sacrificed many of his followers in the past. Perhaps they were simply two more to add to the pyre.'

Rage sniffs. 'You think the doc told me to kill Pearse and Conall in order to win your trust?'

'I would not put it past him,' Owl Man says.

Rage nods thoughtfully. 'You know what? I wouldn't either. He's mad enough to have put me up to it, no doubt about that.'

'So?' Justin asks when Rage doesn't continue. 'Why should we trust you?'

Rage shrugs. 'I don't have an answer for that. You'll take me at face value or you won't. Nothing I say can influence you, so I'm not going to tie myself up in knots trying to convince you that I'm on your side.'

'What does Becky think?' Dan-Dan asks slyly.

'It's a plot,' I tell him. 'Rage is the doc's inside man. If I was you, I'd set a fire in one of the chimneys and chuck him down it.'

'What a splendid idea,' Dan-Dan applauds, his face lighting up. 'I must try that. Not with Michael, but perhaps with one of my other subjects. Make a note, Coley, and remind me later.'

Justin grunts, unamused. 'I want you to keep a

close watch on your new friend, Daniel. If he steps out of line, I'll hold you responsible.'

'Understood,' Dan-Dan salutes.

Justin's gaze settles on me again. 'I underestimated you before, Miss Smith. On the *Belfast* I saw you only as a source of entertainment. I realised my mistake when Dr Oystein and his Angels descended upon us. They would not have risked their lives for an ordinary team member.'

'The doc would have come after any of his Angels,' I disagree.

'No,' Justin says. 'He would not have risked all for the sake of one. There is something different about you. Zachary and Josh have filled me in on some of your history since you resurfaced.'

Zachary is one of the names that Owl Man likes to use. His real name is Tom White, but he prefers a series of aliases.

'You are a resourceful young lady,' Justin goes on, 'with more lives than a cat and a knack for wriggling out of the stickiest of situations.'

'I wouldn't call it a knack,' I mutter. 'Just dumb

luck and a lot of help from people I wouldn't have expected it from.' I nod at Owl Man. 'He's let me go when it would have been easier to kill me. And Josh set me free when I was trapped underground. I still don't know why.' I look at him questioningly.

Josh sighs. 'I took pity on you.'

'You pitied a monster?' Vicky snorts.

'She didn't seem particularly monstrous that day,' Josh says quietly. 'When the other revitaliseds turned on one of their own, she clung to the last shreds of her humanity, even though she knew it meant her end. I figured she deserved better than to be toasted like a marshmallow. I don't regret what I did. I'd do it again if the circumstances were the same.'

'Then we'll be keeping a close eye on you too,' Justin says gruffly. 'Sympathy for one's enemies is a dangerous thing.'

'But she doesn't have to be an enemy,' Dad wheezes, and I can tell it took a lot for him to break his silence. He squirms as the others turn to look at him. 'She can work with us,' he says hoarsely. 'She's not a normal zombie. We can learn things from her. We can use her. If she cooperates . . .'

'I'd say that's a rather strong *if*,' Justin interrupts.

Dad gulps. 'She's my daughter. I know her better than you do. Her head's been turned by the people she got mixed up with. I can explain the reality of the situation to her. When she sees what we're trying to do, I'm sure she'll want to help.'

'Don't you dare speak for me,' I shout. 'You know nothing about me. I was never the person you thought I was.'

Dad smiles shakily. 'Children always think that their parents don't understand them. Trust me, sir. I have faith in her. She can be an asset.'

'And if she refuses to heed your advice?' Justin asks softly. 'If she challenges our right to rule and seeks to bring us down?'

Dan-Dan cracks his knuckles. 'He's got a point, Todd.'

Dad trembles, then steadies himself and grows a pair. 'I'm loyal to the cause,' he says, raising his voice for the first time since we entered the room. 'Nobody can doubt that. I've given my all, done everything that has been asked of me and more. I believe in our mission completely.

'I lost my daughter when she was turned into a zombie. I want her back. She's my flesh and blood, and I love her. But if she won't listen to me . . . if she sets herself against us . . . if she truly is our enemy . . .' His face goes flat. 'Then I'll help Lord Wood dispatch her.'

'That's my dear old dad,' I sneer, trying to burn him alive with my gaze. 'What a jerk.'

'Yes,' Dan-Dan giggles, leaning forward to pat my father's back. 'But he's *our* jerk. Tell me, Becky, what's it like to be betrayed by your closest living relative?'

'Ask your mother and brother,' I murmur. 'Oh, I forgot, you can't — you threw them to the zombies.'

Dan-Dan's expression is darker than I could have hoped for, but it doesn't give me any real satisfaction, because right now I feel abandoned by the one person who should have more reason than any other to stand by me. It doesn't matter that I have such a low opinion of him. He's still my father, and for him to take their side against mine . . .

It hurts.

It hurts like hell.

FIVE

I'm escorted to a lower level. Josh, Owl Man and his dog, Dan-Dan and my dad come with me. Rage tags along as well. And of course we're shadowed by Coley, keeping a close watch on me from behind his sunglasses, taser always at the ready.

'Don't you just love this place?' Dan-Dan says as we pause by a railing to look down on the massive courtyard.

'It's peachy,' I say sarcastically. 'I especially like all the prisoners in the pens.'

'Dull, everyday people,' Dan-Dan snorts. 'You

shouldn't bother yourself with such drab creatures. The world won't miss them.'

'Because they're not white?' I ask icily.

'That has nothing to do with it,' he says, surprising me. 'I actually prefer the world with a bit of colour in it.'

I frown. 'You're not a racist?'

'Perish the thought,' he tuts. 'I only despise weak, boring people, be they white, black or any shade between.'

'How does that fit in with your plans for a super race?' I ask Dad.

He shrugs. 'Lord Wood has been of great assistance to the cause.'

'So it doesn't matter that he's not a bigot?'

'Life makes strange bedfellows of many of us,' Owl Man answers with a wry smile. 'Your father, Daniel, Josh and I have vastly differing views of the world, and our goals are not the same. But we work together because we need one another.'

'And it doesn't trouble you?' I press, nodding at the dejected prisoners in the pens below.

Owl Man sighs and scratches Sakarias's head. The dog whines happily. 'This is a harsh world. I gave up caring about injustices long ago, when I realised I could do nothing to stop them.'

'That's cowardice,' I sneer. 'If you see something wrong, you've got to try to set it right. Otherwise you're as bad as those you hate.'

'But I don't hate anyone,' Owl Man says. 'I would need to hold myself morally superior in order to look down my nose at others. I don't. In my own odd way I'm trying to do some good before I pass on, but I don't think that makes me better than anyone else.'

I laugh cynically. 'What *good* are you trying to do?'

'Come,' he says quietly. 'I will show you.'

Owl Man takes the lead and guides us through a series of rooms which serve as his laboratory. There's equipment everywhere, scientists working on all sorts of experiments. It's like something out of a sci-fi film. Makes Dr Oystein's lab in County Hall look like a chemistry set.

Thinking about the doc, I remember what he told us about Owl Man, how he stole a substance called

Schlesinger-10, a virus which could wipe out every living human if released. Dr Oystein said it was a milky-white liquid. As far as he knew, Owl Man gave the stolen sample to Mr Dowling, but I wonder if he maybe kept some of it for himself. I look for anything that might be the virus as we pass from one room to another, but there are thousands of vials and bottles stored on shelves and most are marked only with complicated symbols. Besides, I doubt that Owl Man would keep such a deadly concoction in open view.

'What's all this for?' Rage asks. 'What are you working on?'

'I have many projects on the boil,' Owl Man says. 'I spend a lot of time working on zombie-related matters, but I'm just as interested in developing cures for the common cold, ways to repair cavities in our teeth, creams to prevent wrinkling in middle-aged ladies.'

'You never told me that,' Dan-Dan says. 'I would be very interested in such a cream. I hate wrinkles. They remind me that I'm getting old, and I'd like to stay young forever, at least in appearance.'

'I'll keep you appraised of developments,' Owl

Man murmurs, and it's hard to tell if he's serious or pulling Dan-Dan's leg. 'But, for all my tinkering, my main focus is the zombie gene. And this is why I have chosen to side with Todd and his kind.'

'It also explains why the army's here,' Josh adds. 'We accept all races in the armed forces, so it's been hard for my colleagues and me to adjust to the current situation. But Zachary has made us a monumental promise and, if he can deliver, it will change everything, so we've had to reluctantly pitch in and lend our backing to people we have little in common with.'

'What promise?' I ask.

'This one,' Owl Man says, pushing a door open and entering a room which is larger than the others. There are lots of medical tables, patients strapped to most, a variety of men and women, with a few children scattered among them. Many of the humans are moaning and writhing. Some are deformed, eyes bulging from their sockets, pus dripping from open wounds, fingers twisted into skeletal shards.

A few of them are zombies, but most seem to be alive, albeit only just. There's a foul odour, partially masked by a strong, sweet scent which is being pumped through the air. All of the scientists are wearing masks and protective clothing.

'Shouldn't we suit up?' Dan-Dan asks, casting a worried glance around.

'You will probably be fine as long as you don't venture too close to any of the guinea pigs,' Owl Man says cheerfully.

'I don't like *probablies*,' Dan-Dan mutters.

Owl Man shrugs. 'You are free to remain outside if you wish.'

Dan-Dan licks his lips and raises an eyebrow at Josh and my father.

'I've been through here plenty of times,' Josh says. 'I haven't suffered any side-effects yet.' He starts to cough alarmingly, then winks to show he's faking.

'At least give me a mask, to help block out the stink,' Dan-Dan grumbles.

'Your wish is my command,' Owl Man murmurs, and masks are duly produced for Dan-Dan, my father and Josh. They don't give one to Coley. He looks uneasy, but doesn't hold back, sticking by my side as charged. I guess he'd rather run the risk of catching a disease than pissing off his child-killing master.

'I was involved in the release of the zombie virus,' Owl Man says as we walk around the room. For a few moments I don't process that. I just nod vaguely. Then the full impact of what he said strikes me and I come to an abrupt halt.

'Did you just admit that the virus was deliberately released?' I gasp.

'Surely you knew that was the case,' Owl Man says. 'You can't have thought that the sudden global outbreak of zombies was random.'

'I knew that dangerous idiots had replicated the virus that Dr Oystein created for the Nazis,' I reply. 'But I thought it had been released accidentally or by terrorists.'

'Terrorists,' Dan-Dan snorts. 'How would any terrorist gain from the downfall of society? Now an anarchist, on the other hand . . .'

'There was no anarchy involved,' Owl Man says smoothly. 'It was carefully calculated by people who knew precisely what they were doing.'

Owl Man stops by one of the restrained zombies

and stares at the mewling creature with an unread-able expression.

'I had no vested interest in the programme,' he says. 'I only wished to be able to continue my experiments. But when I saw which way the wind was blowing, I sided with those who would clearly have the power when the situation shifted.'

'Who were they?' I ask numbly. 'The members of the Board?'

'Among others,' he nods. 'There were all sorts of people who were keen for the zombie revolution to progress smoothly and swiftly. Men of wealth like Justin Bazini, politicians like Vicky Wedge, soldiers like ...' He stops. 'I was about to say Josh, but you were not part of this, were you?'

'No,' Josh says tightly. 'I'm just trying to clean up the mess. I would never have involved myself with anything so insane.'

'If only others in your position had felt the same way,' Owl Man sighs.

'I don't get it,' I mutter. 'Why release the virus? They've ruined everything.'

'That's not how they see it,' Owl Man says. 'The world was in chaos. Too many people draining its natural resources. Global warming. Pollution. Wars that served no purpose. The population needed pruning. They tried other ways, but nothing could offer as swift and sure a result as the release of the zombie virus.

'The timing was far from ideal. I urged them to wait another ten or twenty years, when we would be better equipped to control the restoration of order once we had opened our Pandora's box. But they were impatient. Their secrets had started to leak. They feared exposure and a public backlash.

'There was no defining meeting, no gathering of leaders, tyrants and business heavyweights. The majority simply arrived at a consensus through a series of phone calls and emails, and it was decided to press ahead. So we shipped samples of the virus around the globe, to every major city, and on the agreed date our operatives uncorked the vials and let the virus work its wicked wonders.

'Bases for our forces had been prepared in advance,

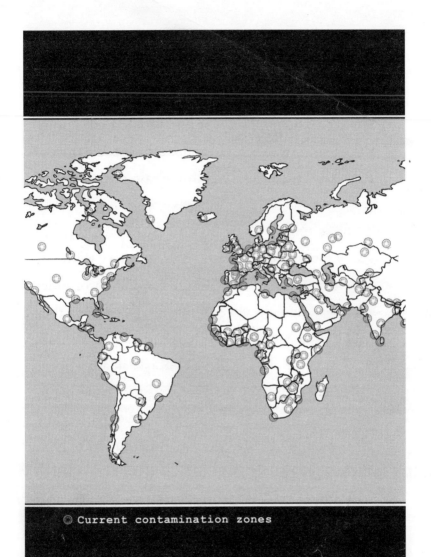

© Current contamination zones

and we moved our troops into them, holding them back until the initial riots had subsided. We also granted sanctuary to leaders who were on our side, wealthy contacts like Justin and Daniel, and others who we felt we might need. Those who hadn't curried favour with us were left to their own devices. I must say, whatever else, we managed to rid the world of a lot of ineffective politicians. For that, if nothing else, we should be thanked.

'While the virus was being released across every continent, more of our operatives disabled satellites and brought the communication networks crashing to their knees. That isolated pockets of humanity, made it difficult for survivors to get in touch with each other. We crippled our own species, removing the tools which would have enabled people to restore order by themselves.

'And that,' he says with a thin smile, 'was how the world ended.'

SIX

I can't believe the matter-of-fact way that Owl Man has broken this news. Rage is surprised too, though he doesn't seem as upset as I am.

'The ageing process was another factor,' Owl Man says as I stare at him wordlessly. 'As Daniel intimated, the rich and powerful do not like to grow old. I suppose most people don't, but when you have more to leave behind, it must be all the harder. To spend a life accumulating great power and wealth, only to be cut off from it all after a mere handful of decades . . .'

'That's why I don't believe in God,' Dan-Dan huffs. 'What sort of a maniac would give us so much, but deny us a decent measure of time to enjoy it? If we were the creation of an ultimate being, He would have bestowed immortality on the leaders of men, the pharaohs, kings and queens, trailblazers like myself.'

'You're too modest,' I growl.

'Truly great men have no need for modesty,' he counters. 'That's a weakness in those who are, for some strange reason, ashamed of their greatness.'

'Many of my experiments are linked to revitalisation,' Owl Man continues, tenderly stroking the cheek of a woman whose tongue is far larger than it should be, sticking out of her mouth like a giant slug caught between her lips. 'Daniel and those like him crave the longevity that is yours, Becky. They would prefer it if we could grant them thousands of years without having to turn them into zombies, but if we can guarantee the restoration of their consciousness, many will settle for an undead existence.'

'Not me,' Dan-Dan says passionately. 'Zombies

can't reproduce. I haven't sired any heirs yet, but I plan to one day.'

'Is that in case you run out of *darlings* to torture and kill?' I taunt him.

Dan-Dan's eyes narrow dangerously, but he says nothing.

'Unfortunately I have not had much success on that front,' Owl Man says as if he hadn't been interrupted. 'There have been advances, and we have come close to a breakthrough several times, but so far it has eluded us.'

'Can't you just give them the same thing that you took?' Rage asks.

'*Took?*' Owl Man rumbles, his features twisting.

'Yeah,' Rage says. 'Whatever you injected yourself with, the strain that gives you some zombie features but not all.'

'I did not inject myself with that foul abomination,' Owl Man says, offended by the suggestion. 'I was content with the natural span of my life. I had no wish to extend it by becoming a semi-living freak.'

'That's not what Dr Oystein told us,' Rage says.

Own Man shrugs. 'The good doctor knows much about my circumstances, but not all. If he thinks that I chose to become this unfortunate creature, torn between the worlds of the living and the undead, he has misjudged me.'

'Then what happened?' Rage asks.

'Mr Dowling,' Owl Man sighs. 'I have worked with him at various times over the years. As I noted earlier, sometimes life sets us up with strange bed-fellows. He is demented but a genius.

'Mr Dowling accepted me as his partner, but he did not approve of my human status. He prefers to sur-round himself with mutants, beings he has converted with his own variations on the zombie virus. I resis-ted his offers to turn me into one of his subhuman beasts, but he would not take no for an answer. He subdued me and infected me with a unique strain. It had killed all of those on whom it had been previously tested. I should have died in agony.'

Owl Man falls silent, his huge eyes distant. Sakarias senses its master's change of mood and licks the back of his hand, trying to restore his spirits. Owl

Man rubs his faithful dog's head, then smiles thinly at me.

'Mr Dowling let me keep a sample of that strain, and I have reproduced it over the years, in an attempt to improve on it. So far I have failed. A few of Daniel's allies have tried it, when they were close to death of natural causes and desperate, but all have perished in great torment.'

'Have any chosen to become mutants?' I ask.

'That option is not open to them,' Owl Man says. 'Mr Dowling has not shared the formulas for his more successful concoctions. I have tried to copy his work, but with limited results.'

'Tell her what our main aim is,' Josh says.

'Yeah,' Dad nods. 'I'm sure she'll see things our way when we explain what we're trying to do.'

'Ever the optimist,' I say witheringly, then cock an eyebrow at Owl Man.

'As I told you a while ago, I wanted to wait before releasing the zombie virus. The main reason was because I hoped to have an antidote in place, which could be distributed among survivors. It would have immunised the living against the virus so, if they were scratched or bitten by a zombie, they would not turn.'

'We could fight them on our own terms then,' Dad says. 'With our superior weapons and brains, we could wipe them out in a matter of weeks.'

'That was the original plan,' Owl Man says. 'Immunise those who were part of the operation, release the virus, let the zombies decimate the ranks of humanity, then immunise the remaining survivors, eliminate the zombies and those we did not care for, sweep away the carcasses and establish a society of our choosing.'

'That was a *good* plan,' Dan-Dan says. 'Like Zachary, I wanted to wait. But Luca, Justin and the others didn't think there was time. There had been leaks. If the masses found out what we were up to, they would have rioted.'

'*I* would have fought them if I'd known,' Josh says sourly.

'So why don't you fight them now?' I challenge him.

He shrugs. 'It's too late.'

'If they were foul then, they're just as foul now,' I insist.

'No argument there,' he says. 'But, as foul as they are, they're the only hope we have at the moment to return control to the living.'

'But they won't do that,' I argue. 'They'll keep control for themselves, crush anyone who isn't the same as them. This will be a world of masters and slaves. Is that what you want?' I nod at the people strapped to the tables. 'Owl Man called them guinea pigs. That's how he sees them. Dan-Dan too. But they're still human in your eyes, aren't they?'

Josh sighs and looks away. 'You can't fight the system,' he croaks. 'Not when the alternative is undead anarchy.'

'That's not the only alternative,' I tell him. 'There's Dr Oystein.'

'Oh yeah,' Rage snorts. 'The guy who believes he's on a mission from God, that Mr Dowling is a representative of the devil. We'd be really safe in *his* hands.'

'Dr Oystein is a good man who only wants the

best for the living,' I say stiffly. 'You know that's true, so don't act like it isn't.'

'You place too much faith in the doc,' Rage jeers. 'But even if he was as good as you believe, do you honestly think he's the one to lead humanity out of the wilderness? He told you all he had to do was kill Mr Dowling to set things right. But it's more complicated than that, isn't it, Owlio?'

'Please don't call me that,' Owl Man says with a pained look.

Rage laughs and waves a hand around at the human subjects. 'This is the only way to fight back if we're serious about stamping out zombies. Personally I don't give a damn. I like things the way they are. The world will be a dull place if these guys get their way. But, if you're as interested in the welfare of the living as you claim, this is the way forward.'

'Not if it involves imprisonment and human experimentation,' I say stubbornly.

'The doc experimented on humans,' Rage reminds me. 'Hell, he experimented on *us*. He didn't ask you for permission when he injected you with the vaccine, did he? Even though he knew you'd probably die young because of it.'

'That was different,' I growl. 'He did it because he had to. But he felt guilty every step of the way. He sometimes had to do bad things, but he would never have thrown in his lot with the Ku Klux Klan and creeps like Dan-Dan.'

Rage cackles bitterly and starts to retort, but I don't let him.

'This is wrong,' I tell everyone, drowning out Rage as he tries to speak again. 'This can never be the right way to go about securing peace. I won't ever side with you monsters.'

'But we need you,' Dad cries. 'We can learn so much from you.'

'It's true,' Owl Man says. 'We have a few revitaliseds, but each one of you is different. The more tests I can run, on as wide a selection as possible, the better our chances of cracking this puzzle.'

'You can help us learn and develop,' Dad says, reaching out to grasp my arms. Then he remembers what I am and stops, frustrated. 'Don't you want to help us find an antidote that will let us win this war? Or something that maybe allows us to restore the brains of those like your mother?'

'Not if it means tyrants like Dan-Dan lording it over people like that,' I sniff, nodding at the nearest shackled victims. 'To be honest, Daddy dearest, I think the zombies would do a better job of running this world than you and your hood-wearing buddies.'

Dad stares at me, stunned. He tries to say something, but is cut short by Dan-Dan. 'You know what this means, don't you?' he booms merrily. When Dad looks at him blankly, Dan-Dan says, 'The minx has turned us down. She won't work with us. That's bad news for humanity.' A shadow passes across his face and he licks his lips sinisterly. 'But good news for Dan-Dan. You're mine now, girl.'

Dad winces, but says nothing to contradict Dan-Dan's claim. Nobody does. And I know, in that instant of appalled silence, that I'm truly, surely doomed.

SEVEN

Dad and Owl Man try to change my mind, but I blank all of their rationalisations, threats and pleas. It's a foolish move. I should play along, win their trust, wait for an opportunity to escape. But I can't be bothered with games and lies. I'd rather stick to my guns and get this over with as swiftly as possible.

When Owl Man sees that I won't budge, he demands my enforced participation in their programme. He wants to chain me up in his lab, so that he can experiment on me at his leisure. But Dan-Dan overrides him. 'She's mine,' he says smugly, pulling rank. Owl Man's furious, but he can't do anything about it.

Coley escorts me back to my cell and locks me up for the night. I'm not too bothered about what lies ahead. I can feel myself coming to the end of my journey, and in many ways it's a relief to be powerless and facing the final curtain. I'm tired of the constant struggle.

The door opens again early in the morning. I wasn't expecting them so soon. I thought Dan-Dan would want to lie in late and make me wait. But I guess he's eager to get started.

My dad has been sent with Coley to collect me. He looks downcast when he enters ahead of the armed guard. Finds it hard to meet my gaze. 'I don't suppose there's any point in asking you to reconsider?' he mumbles.

'Nope,' I say brightly.

He frowns. 'You sound like you're looking forward to this.' When I grin at him, he snaps, 'You're not a martyr. You won't achieve anything by letting them tear you apart. It's a pointless waste.'

'Not entirely pointless,' I smirk. 'It'll make you feel bad.'

'You reckon?' he sneers.

'Of course. You're leading your own child to her torture and execution. You've put your racist hatred before your duty to your daughter. That's gonna eat away at you worse than any cancer ever could.'

'And that makes you happy, does it?' he spits. 'You're willing to throw away your existence just to hurt me?'

'You don't get it, Dad,' I sigh. 'It's not that I want you to suffer. I want to redeem you. Regardless of everything else, you're my father and I love you. I always hoped you'd change, that you'd put the bigotry and bullying behind you, and become an ordinary, nice, loving dad. That was all I ever wanted.

'You let me down,' I continue softly. 'It wasn't all bad. There were times when you shone like a star, like when you came to rescue me at school. But your mean streak always crept back in. It's led you to this, where you're going to willingly walk me to my execution.'

'That's not my fault,' he says. 'It didn't have to go this way. You chose this.'

'Yeah,' I nod. 'But you chose your path too. You could have stood up for me last night. You could have fought them, or at least said you'd leave in disgust if they handed me over to Dan-Dan. Even if you didn't agree with what I was doing, you could have taken my side.

'But you didn't. And you're fine with that now, a good soldier, doing what you're told.' I smile sadly. 'But I think guilt will gnaw away at you. And I'm hoping it will make you question your life and the creeps you've committed it to. If you come good, and strike back at them because you hate them for what they made you do to me, then this won't all have been for nothing.'

Dad shakes his head. 'That won't happen. You're an ignorant girl who doesn't understand the ways of the world. I'd do anything I could to save you, but if you throw yourself off the edge of a cliff . . . Well, what sort of a fool would I be if I leapt after you?'

'A loving fool,' I tell him softly.

Dad scowls, starts to argue with me again, then grunts angrily. 'Come on,' he says. 'We've wasted enough time. Lord Wood is waiting.'

I step out of my cell, Coley following close behind. Dad edges in front of me and guides me up a few flights of stairs to Dan-Dan's quarters. He knocks on the door – a huge wooden door with studs in it, like you find in castles – and it's opened by a young boy, no more than eight or nine years old.

'Who is it, Ciarán?' Dan-Dan calls.

'Todd Smith,' Dad says when the boy looks at him questioningly. 'I'm bringing my daughter to him, as arranged.'

'Todd Smith,' the boy shouts.

'How wonderful,' Dan-Dan purrs, trotting into sight. He's wearing a foil spacesuit, silver boots and gloves, every last bit of him covered, holding a domed helmet under one arm.

'Off on a voyage to the moon?' I quip.

'It seemed appropriate,' Dan-Dan giggles, twirling for my benefit. 'After all, I do recall promising on the

Belfast to put you through a *universe* of torment when I finally got my hands on you.'

Dan-Dan puts on the helmet and steps in front of me, closer than he dared come when I could have sunk my fangs into him. He stares at me hungrily from behind his tempered glass visor. I have nothing to lose, so I quickly snap my neck back then head-butt him. He falls away from me, yelping, but the glass holds.

Coley zaps me with his taser and I collapse in a pain-wracked huddle. Dad bends to help me. Then he remembers that I'm the enemy and he straightens again.

'I knew you'd do that,' Dan-Dan chuckles, getting to his feet. 'I would have been disappointed if you hadn't. It shows you're up for a fight. That's good. You wouldn't be nearly as much fun if you were coming to this broken and spiritless. I love it when they struggle.'

Dan-Dan faces my dad and purses his lips. 'Your loyalty is a lesson for us all, Todd. Many talk the talk, but few walk the walk. I know this can't be easy, but

you've stayed true to your beliefs, putting the welfare of the collective before your own. In my eyes you're a hero.'

Dad shuffles his feet and grins goofily.

'You can stay if you want,' Dan-Dan adds softly. 'I'm happy to let you observe or take part.'

Dad stares at Dan-Dan, then at me, lying in a ball on the floor. He gulps and I see the first flicker of horror dart across his face. But he blinks it away before it can take hold.

'Thank you, my Lord, but I have duties elsewhere which I must attend to.'

'Of course,' Dan-Dan smiles and shows Dad to the door.

Dad pauses before leaving, to look back at me one last time. 'Will you spare her if she changes her mind?' he croaks.

'No,' Dan-Dan says shortly. 'She had her chance and she spurned it. An offer made under duress would be hollow and worthless.'

Dad flinches again, but nods weakly and lets himself be pushed out of the room.

Dan-Dan shuts the door, leans his helmeted head against it and stands there for a while, savouring the last few moments of calm. Then he turns and sets his sights on me. His eyes glitter greedily. His lips are peeled back and his teeth are bared.

'It begins,' he whispers, and oozes towards me like a foil-wrapped nightmare.

EIGHT

Coley pulls on his gloves, grabs me by my feet and drags me through Dan-Dan's chambers. I catch brief glimpses of his living quarters, flowery furniture, scatter cushions everywhere, costumes on mannequins, hardcore images pinned to the walls. I'm surprised he exhibits them so openly. Then again, he has nothing to hide any more. There are no lawyers or police to crack down on him.

Coley and Dan-Dan pick me up and chain me to a large metal table in the middle of the most sparsely decorated room. Grooves run along the edges of the table, draining into buckets. It takes me only a fraction of a second to clock that they're there to catch my blood.

Once I'm secure – I'm bound so tightly that I can't even wriggle – Coley withdraws and takes up position by the door, in case I somehow break free. Dan-Dan checks the chains one last time, then calls, 'Come, my darlings. Look what Dan-Dan has for you.'

Several sullen children trudge into the room. They're dressed finely, their hair is cut immaculately and they've all been made up to look their best, even the boys. But every one of them has the expression of a lost, frightened refugee. The oldest can't be more than ten or eleven.

'Sit on the cushions,' Dan-Dan tells them and they obey sluggishly. 'Keep your eyes on me like I've taught you.' He makes sure they're all doing as instructed. 'Good. I'm proud of you, my darlings. There will be a treat at the end. Although many would think that being privy to such a scene is treat enough.'

Dan-Dan strolls round the table, smiling at me from behind his visor. He waves like a clown. 'Cooee!' When there's silence, he glances over his shoulder, annoyed. The children laugh mechanically.

'Let them go,' I mutter. 'Don't make them watch this.'

'But it's important that I keep them here,' he purrs. 'It's educational. I love my darlings. It's what people like you don't understand. You judge me by the corpses I leave behind. But I'm always trying to save them. I want them to be like me, to appreciate the world the way I do. If I can turn their delicate minds and hearts, I can spare them.'

'Meaning you only spare the wicked?' I sneer.

'I spare the pure,' he counters. 'There's no pure goodness in this world so, rather than waste my time searching for it, I seek out pure evil.' He giggles. 'I don't expect you to understand. Few do. And that's fine. I don't look for sympathy in this life. I'm content to plough my path alone.'

'You're nuttier than a squirrel's stocking on Christmas Day.'

Dan-Dan howls with laughter. 'Even at this late stage, in such a dire position, you persist with the stinging jibes. I'll miss you, Becky. You're a bright spark in a drab world. What a shame I didn't get my hands on you when you were alive.'

He reaches out and strokes my cheek with a gloved finger. I snap at it, hoping to bite through the protective material, but he keeps it just out of my reach.

'Naughty,' he tuts, then turns and heads to the rear of the room. He rolls out a trolley which I hadn't noticed before and pushes it over to the table.

There are shelves on the trolley loaded with knives, axes, saws, hammers, nails, chisels, scissors and more. There are also lots of bottles and tubes filled with liquids and ointments. A drill hangs from a hook and an electric saw from another.

'Those are for when I get lazy,' Dan-Dan says, noting the direction of my gaze. 'You won't have to worry about them for a while. Not for hours, maybe even days, depending on how long I decide to keep you going.' He leans over and leers at me. 'I could string it out for months if I wished. But I think impatience will get the better of me. You'd better hope that it does.'

Dan-Dan sets to work. I don't think he's had a chance to torture a revitalised before, because he begins way too softly. I'm less sensitive than living humans. My nerve-endings are a mess. His early efforts – sticking pins in me, slicing a knife across my flesh, swinging a hammer lightly at my kneecaps, searing the soles of my feet – don't even yield a yelp.

'What a pity,' he sighs, taking a break. 'Torture is an art form, but you seem to be impervious to my more subtle strokes.'

'Sorry to disappoint you,' I grunt.

He shrugs. 'No matter. It just means skipping the build-up and diving in at the deep end. Tell me, Becky, did it hurt a lot when those bones broke through the flesh of your fingers and toes?'

'I can't remember.'

'Well, let's see if it hurts when I try hammering them back in,' he chuckles, reaching for a small sledgehammer.

The pain isn't that bad, but the noise of my

shattering bones really unsettles me. I start to think that there can't be anything worse. Then Dan-Dan stops, studies my feet and says, 'I wonder what would happen if I tried to pull the bones out instead of driving them in?'

And I realise that, when it comes to the world of torture, I'm an innocent. I've so much to learn. But I'm going to find out soon.

Dan-Dan reaches for a pair of pliers. He snaps them open and shut a few times, then whistles as he sets to work on my fingerbones.

Our delirious dance of destruction picks up pace.

NINE

I'm no expert, but Dan-Dan seems damn good at this, curse his soul. I suppose he's had lots of practice over the years. He was a notorious child-killer in the old days, back when he ran the risk of being captured and jailed, and he's had a completely free run at it since society fell.

He prods and pokes with nails until he finds the areas where I can still be hurt. He peels flesh from my bones in the most excruciating places, then rubs salt and acidic liquids into the wounds.

It isn't long before I'm screaming at the ceiling,

straining against my bonds, cursing Dan-Dan for putting me through this most unholy of hells.

'Shush, my lovely,' Dan-Dan soothes me. 'We're only getting started. It's too soon for screams of that nature. Save them for when you *really* feel the pain.'

He tries several times to pull out the bones from my fingers and toes, but they resist his efforts. Finally he sets about pulping them with a hammer and chisel. When he's destroyed the bits sticking out, he digs away at the bones inside. When that fails to have much of an impact, he moves on to more profitable zones.

He has great fun exploring the gaping hole where my heart should be. He scrapes away the moss and opens up dried valves, letting thick, soupy blood flood the cavity. Then he soaks it up with a sponge and squeezes it over my face, drenching me with my own foul gore.

The blood trickles from my cheeks and flows slowly across the table, along the grooves and into the buckets, which have been collecting every drop that

Dan-Dan has wrung from me. My best hope is that he drains too much and my brain shuts down. But I don't think undead bodies work that way. Zombies can survive if their heads are cut off, so I guess the flow of blood to the brain isn't as crucial as it is in the living.

Dan-Dan chats away to me the whole time, telling stories, teasing me, sharing dark secrets. Sometimes he whistles. Other times he sings. He's only occasionally silent, and then it's purely for effect, when he wants me to hear nothing except my own screams or panting sobs.

Some of his darlings cry and flee the room. Dan-Dan always sends the others to drag them back. There is to be no escape for any of us here tonight.

Coley is replaced by a couple of soldiers after a few hours, and they in turn are replaced a few hours after that. I guess normal people don't have the stamina for this that Dan-Dan does.

It grows dark and he stops to eat, his first meal of the long, blood-drenched day. He retires to a corner of the room and carefully removes his helmet. He barks an order at the soldiers on duty and they help him out of the spacesuit.

Dan-Dan settles himself on a plump cushion and a few of his darlings feed him, dropping chunks of food into his mouth, the way that Coley fed my mother when I was taken to see her. His suit, drenched with my blood, lies in a heap nearby. I want to call to the children, tell them to dip a nugget in the blood and slyly finish him off. But I can't make any sounds at the moment except for a thin, wheezing noise. Dan-Dan cut through to my vocal cords before he stopped to eat, and pinched them shut with something.

'This is exhausting,' Dan-Dan sighs, getting to his feet after the meal and stretching. 'I need a rest. Sing to me, my darlings, and help me sleep for a while.'

The children gather a load of the cushions and make a bed. Dan-Dan lies back and they encircle him. They kneel and sing a lullaby. Dan-Dan smiles and wags a finger at them like a conductor. His eyelids start to droop. Before they close, he jerks fully awake and snaps at a soldier, 'Don't forget to empty out the suit while I slumber.'

'Yes, my Lord,' the soldier says.

'There's a waste system inside it,' Dan-Dan explains for my benefit. 'Just like a real spacesuit. That's why I've been able to work without having to stop for minor inconveniences.'

Dan-Dan lies back again and the children croon from the beginning of the lullaby. Soon he's snoring and twitching as he dreams. The children keep on singing until they start to doze off themselves. As they tire, they lie down around him. In the end only one remains at his post, a pale boy, eight or nine years old. It's Ciarán, the child who let me into Dan-Dan's quarters. He carries on singing in a soft, cracked voice. By the pained look on his face, I don't think he stays awake because he wants to. I think he's just afraid of what he'll dream about when he falls asleep.

TEN

Dan-Dan doesn't snooze for more than a couple of hours. Then he rises and re-suits, and the torture continues through the night. He breaks a few times to catch forty winks and refresh himself, but otherwise shows an almost zombie-like lack of a need to sleep.

As the night drags on, his darlings can't keep their eyes open, and eventually all of them pass out, even little Ciarán. Dan-Dan doesn't try to wake them, accepting their limitations.

'Aren't they sweet?' he says at one point, taking a

break to let me recover ahead of the next assault. 'I love watching them like this. Such a shame that they have to wake. Sometimes I smother them in their sleep, to preserve that sweet look on their faces.'

'I hope one of them returns the favour some day,' I mutter weakly. He has unpinched my vocal cords, so I have my voice back, but speaking is an effort. I'm starting to seriously flag. I've lost so much blood and my energy has drained away. It's hard to even wriggle my toes or fingers. But, although Dan-Dan can break my body, he'll never break what beats deep inside me. I'll carry on cursing him as long as I have a tongue in my head.

'Becky, Becky, Becky,' Dan-Dan sighs, removing his helmet to draw a few breaths of fresh air. 'Why do you goad me? If you simply accepted me as your god of torment and begged me to finish you off, I could be merciful.'

I chuckle painfully. 'You want me to call you a god now?'

'That's what I am to you,' he says. 'I'm everything, just as a real god is to his followers. I control your life completely. I can free you from your pain or drag it out endlessly. Worship me, Becky. Show me the respect which I am due. If you do, I will grant you the release that I'm sure you long for.'

'Get stuffed, fat man,' I snort.

Dan-Dan shakes his head. 'You're a worthy adversary. I almost feel sorry for you. I'm half-tempted to bring proceedings to an abrupt conclusion.'

'No you're not,' I wheeze. 'You're just saying that to give me hope, so that you can squash it. I'm wise to all your tricks.'

Dan-Dan laughs. 'Thank heaven the rest of my darlings are not as insightful as you. This would be a joyless existence if everyone could see through me the way you can.'

My tormentor replaces his helmet and circles the table again. He's been doing that all day and night, a coldly cruising shark. I stare at the ceiling and tense myself for whatever he has lined up next.

'Such a pitiful-looking body,' he murmurs, running the tip of a knife across the exposed flesh of my stomach and over my ribs. I've been naked for a long time. Dan-Dan cut away my clothes several hours ago. I think he expected me to be more bothered by that, but the undead aren't modest like the living.

'I wonder how many of these you can do without?' Dan-Dan says, tapping the ribs. 'I think it's time to find out.'

He starts cutting the flesh away from over my ribs, then begins snapping off bits of them. I scream abuse at him and the children stir, but Dan-Dan ignores me and continues, not stopping until a large section of my ribcage has been pruned back to its stumps and most of my inner organs are in open view.

Dan-Dan rests for a while. He calms his darlings and dozes in their company. I lie on the table, panting and wide-eyed, my withered lungs exposed as I listen to him snore. There have been many times since I regained my senses when I've wished that I could cry, but never more so than tonight. Tears wouldn't help, but at least they'd give me some small form of release.

Dan-Dan sleeps for three or four hours this time. Finally he stirs, has a bite to eat and returns to his station. I expect him to be groggy, but he's as bright-eyed as ever. He begins rooting around, focusing on my freshly revealed guts, finding new ways to make me wince, shriek and shudder.

As the sun rises and natural light floods the room, I start to hallucinate. I begin to think that Dan-Dan is a real spaceman, that I'm on a rocket bound for the stars. I welcome the hallucinations and try to run with them, to lose myself in the world of fantasy. But Dan-Dan sees what's happening and eases off, waiting for my senses to return to normal.

'The brain is a fascinating organ,' he says cheerfully when he's sure that I can understand his words. 'Everything is wired back to it. All that we feel or experience is determined by what our brain tells us. If you could convince your brain not to acknowledge the signals sent by your nerve-endings, I couldn't hurt you. If I cut off your legs, a few centimetres at a time, you'd simply lie there and laugh at me.

'I've dug around in plenty of brains,' he continues, 'but they're too complex for my liking. More often than not I've accidentally destroyed cells which have made my subjects immune to many of my torments.

'Don't worry, Becky,' he smiles. 'I won't go near your brain until the end. I want you conscious and responsive every step of the way. If I see you starting to veer out of this realm, I'll do all that I can to haul you back.'

'Too ... considerate ... of ... you,' I whisper.

Dan-Dan laughs and returns to work. He takes it easier now, leaving my more vulnerable sections alone, happy to just teasingly poke at me for a while, letting me swim back to full awareness.

The children wake up. Dan-Dan orders breakfast for them and they tuck in numbly as they watch him chip away at me. Their eyes are bleary and unfocused. They want this to end. It's an ordeal for them. I wish I could grant them their longed-for finale, but Dan-Dan holds all the trump cards and he's not going to play them until he's well and truly done with me.

The morning stretches on, becomes afternoon, night, then morning again. I start to lose track of time. Has it really only been forty-eight hours since I was brought to Dan-Dan's quarters, or have I been here for weeks? Maybe it's been months, and I've blanked out huge chunks of time in order to stay sane.

As the sun rises again and the children play some sort of clapping game to keep themselves distracted, Dan-Dan cuts off the tops of my ears. The pain isn't that great, but he holds up a mirror for me and cackles with delight at my dismayed expression.

'You'll have trouble wearing sunglasses now,' he hoots. 'Not that you're ever going to need them again.' He pauses and steps back to study his handiwork. 'Is it time?' he mutters.

I cock my head, wondering if he's tired of me, if he's finally going to draw things to a close.

Dan-Dan picks up a surgical knife and points the tip at my left eye. I squeal and try to thrash my head aside, but it's locked in place. He laughs and grabs my chin. Waves the tip of the knife in front of my eye. Pokes my eyeball slowly, agonisingly . . .

Then he stops. 'No,' he frowns. 'The trouble with

blinding is that it removes a lot of other options. I save it for when I'm absolutely certain that there's nothing else I want to try. We're not at that stage yet. Close, but not quite.

'We've forgotten something, Becky, something important. We've been so focused on our fun and games that we've overlooked all other concerns. There was unfinished business that we should have dealt with before I brought you here, but I can't for the life of me remember what it was.'

He steps back and scratches the chin of his helmet, pulling a confused expression. It's all a show. He knows exactly what it is that he has pretended to forget. This is no random interruption. I'm sure it's something he's been planning since the start. I can tell by the cunning, self-satisfied twinkle in his eyes.

I've no idea what Dan-Dan has been holding back until this late stage, and to be honest I don't care. Rather than try and think one step ahead of him, I lie still and wait for him to play out his childish game, figuring it can't be any worse than what he's already subjected me to.

'What can it be?' he murmurs. 'What could be so pressing that I feel the need to stop? Any ideas, Becky?' I don't respond, just stare at the ceiling. 'Darlings? Can you be of help?' The children shake their heads, mute with terror. 'Coley!' he barks at the guard who has resumed his station. 'What have I forgotten?'

'I don't know, my Lord,' Coley answers, playing along, but I can tell by his vicious grin that he's in on the joke.

'This is so frustrating,' Dan-Dan cries. 'We can't continue until I sort this out. I'm sure it was something major. If I could just think clearly for a few seconds . . .'

Dan-Dan strides to the back of the room and squats in a fake huff. He stays there for a couple of minutes while I stew on the table. Then he shouts, 'Aha!' Springing to his feet, he hurries back and bends over me, waving his hand until I give him my attention. 'I've remembered. I can't believe we forgot. How easily distracted we are.'

Then, as I'm staring at him with exhausted contempt, Dan-Dan leans in close and purrs slyly, 'What on earth has happened to *Vinyl*?'

ELEVEN

Dan-Dan tells Coley to bandage over what's left of my guts, to hold them in place. Then he frees my head and tries to feed me chunks of brain. I keep my lips closed until he shrugs and says, 'Well, if you'd rather I just ordered Vinyl's execution . . .'

Bizarrely, I'd forgotten my main reason for coming to the Power Station, to secure Vinyl's release and to try to get the other New Kirkham prisoners freed with him. Killing Dan-Dan would have been a welcome bonus, but getting Vinyl and his people out of here was my first priority. With the shock of finding my dad alive, and then with everything I've suffered at Dan-Dan's hands, that had been shaken from my thoughts. But now that I've remembered, I feel compelled to do whatever I can to help.

Reluctantly, knowing it will give me the energy to endure for longer, I open my mouth and accept the scraps which Dan-Dan drops my way. I chew sluggishly, forcing myself to swallow. Even that small movement is painful. I retch up the first few pieces almost immediately, before I'm able to draw nutrients from them, but Dan-Dan patiently feeds me again and this time the food stays down long enough for me to absorb the nourishment which I need to continue.

Dan-Dan treats me to all the brains that I can stomach, then heads out and leaves me alone for a while, giving me time to digest my meal. I don't manage to throw up all of the cranial chunks, but that doesn't matter. Normally I'd be worried about attracting bugs which would lay eggs inside me, but I don't think I'll live long enough to become an all-night diner for the creatures of the insect world.

Dan-Dan's gone for ages. He took the children with him, and Coley has stepped out too, though I'm sure he's stationed nearby, ready to rush in if he hears anything untoward.

Despite the loss of blood, I feel some of my strength returning. It's not a welcome sensation. Fresh pain flares all over as muscles twitch and my body processes the nutrients. I groan softly and bang my head against the table to drive the worst of the agony from my brain. I pause and think about trying to crack my skull open. But, even as I'm wondering if I could do that, Coley reappears and slips a cushion beneath my head.

'There,' he smiles. 'That's far more comfortable, isn't it?'

He must have been told to listen out for the noise. Dan-Dan saw the opportunity before I did and took steps to ensure I didn't rob him of his fun prematurely.

I scowl at the smirking guard. 'If you were halfway human,' I croak, 'you'd finish me off before that monster returned.'

'Do you think I'm mad?' Coley retorts. 'I'd end up where you are if I lifted a finger to help you.'

'It's not such a bad place to be,' I sigh. 'I'd rather die doing the right thing than live and serve a twisted beast like Dan-Dan.'

Coley's smile fades and he studies me seriously. 'Barnes thought that way too. But I don't.' He pulls a face. 'I can't.'

'You're a sad case, Coley,' I whisper, and for once I'm not insulting him.

'Maybe,' he nods. 'But come tomorrow, I'll be alive and you'll be history.'

'But what are you living for?' I challenge him. 'What are you living *as*?'

'I try not to think about that,' Coley says softly, then returns to his post outside the room.

When Dan-Dan returns – back in his beloved sailor's outfit – there are several soldiers with him. He tells Coley to unshackle me and help me to my feet. Dan-Dan keeps in the background, directing proceedings from afar. He encourages me to exercise gently and limber up. I do as he says, knowing there's no point rebelling, as he'll simply play the Vinyl card if I get mutinous.

I cry out with pain as I swing my arms back and forth. I collapse to my knees and have to be helped back to my feet by Coley. Cursing softly, I try again, and this time I manage to stay upright, although the blisters on the soles of my feet mean that even standing still is a torment, and the missing toe bones make balancing a tricky act — I'd grown to depend on them and feel strange without them.

'Good,' Dan-Dan beams. 'You're the most resilient specimen I've ever crossed paths with. Do some squats for me, Becky.'

I shoot him the finger and he laughs. I continue working out the kinks as slowly and carefully as I can. Each tiny gesture sets off bursts of pain somewhere within me, but I grit my teeth and carry on.

A couple of the soldiers remove the buckets as I'm exercising, taking them off to do who knows what with my blood. If I was human, I wouldn't be surprised if Dan-Dan filled a bath with the thick liquid to bathe in. But of course he can't, as one drop of it

on his skin would be enough to turn him into a mindless, undead beast.

'How are you feeling?' Dan-Dan asks.

'Like I'm ready to run a marathon,' I growl.

'Incredible,' he sighs. 'Two full days and nights of taking all that I can throw at you, and you still haven't cracked. I think I might have got you up from your deathbed too early. Maybe I'll strap you down for another few rounds before we go looking for Vinyl.'

I don't respond to that. I'm pretty sure he's saying it just to tease me, but I'm concerned that if I wind him up he might follow through on the threat.

As I'm working the worst of the stiffness out of my limbs, Dad appears behind Coley and Dan-Dan. His face falls when he spots me. My flesh has been sliced up, peeled away and burnt to blackened shreds. Dan-Dan shaved off the last of my hair early in the process and drove a few nails into the crown of my head, which he has left in place. He pulled out some of my teeth, and of course he cut off my ears.

'*B?*' Dad gasps, not entirely sure I'm the daughter

he left in the care of Lord Daniel Wood just two short days ago.

'I hope you're proud of what you've helped reduce me to,' I mumble, raising my arms and giving him a slow twirl. He can't see my dismantled ribcage and hacked-up guts through the bandages, but Dan-Dan also sawed off my right breast – I've done my best to erase the scene from my memory, so I can't recall when exactly he came up with that particular brain-wave – and the gaping sore is uncovered, as is the seeping hole in the left side of my chest.

Dad stares at me with horror, then turns his gaze on Dan-Dan.

'What?' Dan-Dan snaps. 'Did you think I was going to smack her bottom and leave it at that?'

Dad gulps. 'No. I knew you'd ... but I didn't think ...'

'It's not as bad as it looks,' Dan-Dan smirks. 'Zombies can't feel as much pain as us. I had to be harsher on her than I would have been on one of the living. She's far from chipper, but she's healthier than she appears.'

'Oh yeah,' I snort. 'Right as rain, me. Don't worry yourself about it, Dad. This is what my kind do for kicks.'

'I'm sorry,' Dad says softly, then hardens his expression, snaps his heels together and salutes Dan-Dan. 'The cage is ready, my Lord. We have chosen the participants in line with your wishes.'

'Very good,' Dan-Dan murmurs. He winks at me. 'I'm looking forward to this, Becky. It should be quite a show.'

I grin ghoulishly. 'I'll try not to disappoint.' I've no idea what he has planned, but I'm sure it will be inventive and nasty. Whatever it is, I won't let it faze me. I'll treat it like it's no big thing, not give him the satisfaction of seeing me tremble.

'Hands behind your back,' Coley barks, stepping forward with cuffs. He's wearing gloves, but his face isn't protected. I think about hurling myself at him, infecting him, forcing the soldiers to open fire. I don't mind if I perish in a hail of bullets, and taking Coley down with me would be a sweet bonus. But if I do that, Vinyl will be killed too. I don't know if I'll be able to help my friend, or if Dan-Dan has rigged the game in such a way that I'm damned to lose no matter what. But if there's a chance that I can win Vinyl's freedom, I have to take it.

So, like an obedient little girl, I put my hands behind my back and let myself be cuffed. Then we file out of the room and march through Dan-Dan's sickly sweet domain. I didn't think I'd ever be coming back this way when I was admitted a couple of days ago. In all honesty, I'm not relieved that I've been given a respite. I'd rather have died on the table, as I was sure I was destined to. It would have been easier that way. Whatever Dan-Dan has lined up for me, it's sure to involve fighting and heartache. How much more do I have to endure before I'm granted my final, much-longed-for release?

TWELVE

I'm taken to the courtyard. It's a grey day and much of the open space is shrouded in shadows, but my eyes still struggle to adjust to the natural light after the gloom of Dan-Dan's room. I want to shield them with a hand, but obviously I can't since they're bound behind my back.

Coley leads me to a large cage in the centre of the yard. I noticed this one before when I passed, because of its size, but didn't take much notice. Unlike most of the cages, it wasn't packed with prisoners.

Now it's different. There are figures inside. As I

draw closer and my eyes focus, I count thirteen people, twelve huddled against one wall of the cage, the thirteenth chained to the bars on the opposite side. The twelve are divided equally, four men, four women, four children — two boys, two girls.

The thirteenth is Vinyl.

Dan-Dan slips ahead of me and opens the door of the cage. Then he stands back as my hands are freed and I'm pushed inside. The door slams shut immediately.

I stagger forward, then take stock. A crowd has gathered, soldiers and Klanners. Owl Man and Josh are among the group behind Vinyl. Unlike most of the others, they're not cheering or clapping. They look solemn and resigned.

Rage takes up a position next to Dan-Dan. At least he gets as close as he's allowed. Dan-Dan must be wary of the traitor, as a couple of his soldiers keep their guns trained on the hulking teenager. Rage doesn't mind. He seems happy as a pig in its sty.

'You did a real job on her,' Rage enthuses, casting an appreciative eye over me.

'I'm a craftsman,' Dan-Dan smiles. 'I take pride in what I do.'

'I bet you wish you'd stayed in County Hall,' Rage calls to me. In reply I drag a finger across my throat then point it at him. But he knows it's an idle threat. He's safe on his side of the bars.

Justin Bazini and Vicky Wedge appear, the crowd parting to let them press up close to the cage. Vicky is grinning eagerly but Justin is frowning.

'Is she in any fit condition to fight?' he growls.

'She'll surprise you,' Dan-Dan assures him. 'There's more to this young firebrand than meets the eye. I pushed her hard but not too far. She'll put on a good show.'

Justin doesn't look convinced, but he grunts and waits for the action to start.

I edge closer to Vinyl. He's been given a going-over since I last saw him, but he doesn't look anywhere near as bad as me. His left eye is puffed up, but he can see out of his right. He nods and says, 'Hey, B.'

'Hey, V,' I smile.

'Some mess we're in, huh?' he sighs.

'Tell me about it.'

'You shouldn't have come back.'

'I know.'

'They'd have killed us no matter what.'

'Not true,' Owl Man says. 'I planned to release you as promised. I was even going to plead for your townsfolk to be set free along with you. Rage is to blame for what has happened — his act of treachery changed everything. I am a man of my word.'

'That's comforting,' Vinyl says drily, then grimaces. 'They really put you through hell. I thought they were tough on me but . . .'

'Don't worry about it,' I wheeze. 'They can't break the B. I've bounced back from worse than this.'

Vinyl raises an eyebrow and I laugh, then wince as pain shoots through me.

'Thanks anyway,' Vinyl says quietly. 'It means a lot, that you tried.'

'Did you think I wouldn't?'

He shrugs, his chains rattling. 'When you're in a situation like this, you start thinking all sorts of things.' He looks over my head at the gathered vultures. 'What are they going to do to us?'

'It'll be some sort of gladiatorial thing,' I guess.

'Me versus you?' Vinyl frowns.

'No. I think they want to pit me against those guys.' I nod at the people being held on the far side of the cage.

'Don't do it,' Vinyl says instantly. 'Some of them are from New Kirkham. Even if they weren't, I wouldn't want to trade my life for all of theirs. Let the buggers kill me.'

'You don't mean that,' I mutter.

'I do,' he insists. 'I'd rather you stood by and let them finish me off. I don't want you to murder on my account. Besides, they'll butcher me in the end, no matter what you do. Isn't that right?' he roars at those around us. 'This is a no-win situation, isn't it?'

'Not necessarily,' Dan-Dan chuckles. 'The ground might open up and swallow you, or angels – real angels, not Becky's group of copycats – might drop from the sky and spirit you away.'

'She won't fight for me,' Vinyl yells. 'Tell them, B.'

I glance uncertainly at Vinyl, then roll my eyes and nod. 'He's the boss. If he says no fighting, so be it.'

Dan-Dan's smile never wavers. 'Such a noble pair,' he trills. 'I admire your resolve. And I think you'd hold firm under normal conditions. I can see why. Only a heartless monster would kill twelve good, harmless people in order to save a friend. But what if they weren't harmless and good?'

Dan-Dan flashes his teeth at me as Coley steps up close to the bars where the prisoners are cowering. Now that I look at them more clearly, I realise they're being held in place by ropes looped round their throats. They can't back away for fear of being choked.

Coley is carrying a bucket that is all too familiar.

'No!' I roar, seeing their plan now. I start to limp across the cage, desperate to stop it, to bargain with Dan-Dan, to reach a compromise. But before I can say anything, Coley dips a ladle into the bucket, dredges up a hefty slug of the blood which seeped from my flesh while I was being tortured, then scatters it across the trapped men, women and children. As I scream at him, he dips the ladle in again, then flicks it at the humans in turn, making sure every one of them catches a few drops.

The doomed victims shriek and moan as my infected blood seeps into their pores, spreading the zombie virus through their bodies. I draw to a halt and watch wretchedly, too late to save them. Even though I'm not responsible for what's about to happen, it's my blood that was used, so I feel like I'm to blame. Twelve more lives to add to my list of shame.

The humans shudder and froth. It's impossible, with all the screaming, to distinguish the ripping sounds as the bones in their fingers and toes lengthen and force their way out through the layers of flesh. But I watch as their teeth extend and their eyes go flat, as they stand, reborn, their nostrils flaring as they fix on the scent of living brains.

'That always freaks me out,' Dan-Dan murmurs. 'It's a beastly business, isn't it?' He shakes his head glumly, then grins. 'I'm sure I don't need to explain the rules to you, Becky. They're going to target your friend. If you don't stop them, they'll rip his brain from its skull and dig in.'

'No,' Vinyl whispers behind me, but he's no longer

asking me to step aside and let him be killed. The game has changed. While he would have gladly sacrificed himself to save twelve living people, he's filled with dread at the thought of being torn apart by a pack of zombies.

'Unleash the hounds of hell!' Dan-Dan squeals, and the men holding the ropes release them. The zombies claw at the bars, snarling hungrily, eager to sink their fangs into the heads of the humans who are laughing at them and cheering.

Then one of the girls catches sight of Vinyl. She realises he's alive and on her side of the bars. She lets out an excited mewling sound. The others turn and bunch round her. They stare at Vinyl. Their lips lift from their long, sharp teeth. Their bone-enhanced fingers flex. Then all twelve of them come loping across the cage, mindless, soulless killing machines on the attack.

THIRTEEN

I'm a physical wreck. Dan-Dan has put me through the wringer over the last forty-eight hours and I'm in no shape to pit myself against a dozen freshly minted zombies. But if I stand aside and let them race past, it's curtains for Vinyl. As drained and wracked with pain as I am, I have to push myself one more time.

My training kicks in and I instinctively look for angles. Revitaliseds usually have the advantage over reviveds in a one-on-one battle, since we have the full use of our mental faculties. But twelve against one is a completely different scenario. It would be a huge challenge at the best of times. Given my sorry state, I have a mountain to climb. But success isn't an impossibility. Master Zhang taught us to look for the positive in any fight and to always believe that victory is ours for the taking.

The zombies aren't paying any attention to me. They see me as one of their own, and the undead don't attack their kin. I can use that to shake them up and lure them away from Vinyl.

My focus settles on the children. I target the smallest girl, shift across until I'm directly in her path, and brace myself. The pack draws abreast of me. The girl tries to veer round. I tackle her, pick her up, grab a leg and arm, then swing her like a scythe, knocking over the nearest zombies, before lobbing her at the others, like throwing a bowling ball at a set of pins.

The reviveds go down in a confused huddle, moaning and roaring with surprise. One of the boys is next to me. He's young, and until a minute ago he was innocent, but I don't think about that. Making a blade of my right hand, I drive my fingers at the side of his head, to break through the covering of bone and destroy the brain within.

'Bloody hell!' I scream as my fingers smash against what feels like a brick wall. As I shake my hand and wince, I remember that Dan-Dan sheared off the bones that I've grown to rely on. They've been deadly weapons in my battles to date. Now they're gone.

'Oh dear,' Dan-Dan hollers. 'Did you forget that you don't have your lovely fingerbones any longer? What now, little girl?'

Ignoring Dan-Dan's heckling, I pick up the boy and throw him at the adult zombies who are getting back to their feet. As they go down in a heap again, I lean over one of the women, open my mouth wide and bite down behind her left ear. Dan-Dan had a swell time chipping away at my teeth and drilling through to the buried nerve-endings, but he only removed a few, and the rest are sharp enough to still be of use.

I rip a chunk of skull away. As the woman shrieks, I dig into her brain with my fingers and jerk them around until she falls still.

One down, eleven to go.

'I should have ground those teeth down to the gums,' Dan-Dan mutters. 'I was too soft on the savage creature.'

'Nonsense,' Justin snorts. 'She must have some means of disabling her opponents, otherwise it would be a one-sided fight, and where's the sport in that?'

'Go on, Becky,' an animated Vicky Wedge cheers. 'Bite, girl, bite!'

I tune out the members of the Board and attack one of the men. I catch him as he's getting to his feet and finish him off the same way as the woman.

The others are upright now and they're no longer focused on Vinyl. Instead they're glaring at me. Reviveds can't understand it when one of us turns against them. Treachery isn't in their nature. But when offended, they're quick to respond to the insult.

All ten of the remaining zombies launch themselves at me. I fall into a ball and roll, knocking a few to the ground, evading the clutches of the others. I need something to strike them with. I can't expect to chew my way through all of their skulls. They won't hold still for me like the first pair.

Master Zhang taught us to look for weapons everywhere. We usually didn't leave County Hall tooled up. Instead we were told to make the most of everyday items that might be lying around. A brick, a spoon, a CD, a pair of glasses ... I could wreak havoc with any of those objects.

The trouble is, the floor of the cage is littered with dust but nothing else. No feeding bowls, no loose chains, no discarded knives. There aren't even any good-sized stones.

One of the men grabs me and jabs at my skull with his fangs. I glimpse a length of rope swinging in front of my eyes and recall how the humans were held in place while they were alive. As I duck my head back and forth, I grab hold of the rope and run my left hand up to where the knot holds the noose in place. I close my fingers into a fist and jam it against the knot. Then, with my right hand, I pull sharply, tightening the noose swiftly and fiercely.

The rope rips through the man's neck and his head

flies from its perch, to hit the ground and tumble through the dirt. There's a huge cheer from the watching humans. They *liked* that move!

As more of the zombies hurl themselves at me, I use the decapitated man's body as a shield. I haven't killed him, but he can't get his bearings without his head, so his arms and legs flail wildly.

I'm backing away, desperately searching for something that might pass as a weapon, when one of the man's hands strikes my cheek. His nails slice into my flesh and open a thin cut. It's only a minor sting, but I pause as a thought strikes.

Hiding my head beneath the man's chest, ignoring the probing fingers of the other zombies, I pull the man's arm in close, bite into his wrist and sever through flesh and bone. As the hand starts to come loose, I rip it free, then push the man back into the huddle of his companions and scrabble clear.

The boy I tried to brain leaps through the air and lands on me, driving me down. He tears at the bandages around my ribcage and starts digging into what's left of my guts. With a scream of pain and fury, I squeeze the fingers of the severed hand together, hold it like a dagger, then drive the bones sticking out of the fingertips through the centre of the boy's forehead.

'Now that's sheer genius!' Dan-Dan whoops as the boy spasms and falls away. 'I told you she'd make a decent fight of it, didn't I?'

'I stand corrected,' Justin laughs. 'What a warrior.'

In an ideal world, I'd stop to toss a quip their way, something along the lines of, *You have to hand it to me!* But there's no time for childish one-upmanship. Eight of the zombies are still active. If I lose my focus for even a second, it will be the end of me.

One of the women rushes me. Raising a foot, I kick the side of her head and make perfect contact. There's a cracking sound and she flies sideways. She doesn't get up again, but squirms like a dying fish. I must have damaged her brain with the blow, not enough to kill her, but to put her out of commission, at least for the immediate future.

A man rugby-tackles me. I hammer an elbow into the middle of his back. It hurts him but he doesn't let go. The rest of the zombies crowd around and suddenly I'm being dragged across the yard in a scrum. I keep pounding at the man and the others, but they don't release me.

Finally we go down in a pack, the zombies losing their balance. It's chaos, and as they lash out at one another, trying to break free of the mess, I grab a woman's skull and sink my teeth in. I break through to the brain, but before I can stab into it, she pulls herself free and the chance to finish her off is lost.

One of the creatures gets a hand inside the hole where my heart used to be and starts scraping at the flesh, opening up wounds which had just begun to heal after Dan-Dan's meddling. Howling, I beat at the hand until it's withdrawn.

Sitting up, I grab the first head that I see – it turns out to be one of the girls – wrap an arm round it and twist until the neck snaps. Pushing the disoriented zombie away, I force myself backwards. I don't get very far before running up against the bars of the cage. The zombies screech with delight – they think they have me cornered – but this is bad news for them. The bars are cold, hard steel. Impossible to wrench free. But I can use their solidity.

A tall black man with dyed orange hair lunges at me. I shimmy aside, grab his shoulders and slam him head first into a couple of the bars. His skulls shatters and he drops.

The woman whose skull I bit through attacks next. Grabbing her head, I slam it into the bars, but she doesn't go down as neatly as the orange-haired man. Grunting, she manages to latch on to my hand and chews into it, drawing another scream from my lips.

The girl with the snapped neck has staggered away from the ruckus as she tries to set her head back in its rightful place. The other girl throws herself on top of me and the woman, getting in the way of the adults who could otherwise have taken advantage of my indisposition to finish me off.

As the girl slaps and tugs at me, the woman continues to grind down. I explore with the fingers of my free hand, find the hole in her head which I had earlier opened up, and try digging in. But the hole's too small. I can't damage enough of her brain to stall her.

One of the men starts to tug the girl away. I only have a few seconds before I'm exposed again. Inserting a lone finger into the hole in the woman's head, I exert pressure and try to snap off another shard of bone. If her skull holds, that will be the end of me. But luck hasn't deserted me entirely. A long sliver of bone snaps off in my hand. It almost slips away from me, but I snatch at it before it drops, get a good grip, then drive it into the woman's brain like a dagger.

As the woman's teeth relax and she slips away, I spin swiftly and drive the bit of bone through the eye of the man closing in on me. It pops the eye and embeds itself in his brain. He shrieks and backpedals, knocking the remaining zombies aside before he collapses and dies.

I shove the girl off and ram her head into the bars. As she drops, I realise to my astonishment that I now have only two zombies to deal with, a woman and a boy. The others are either dead or incapacitated.

I stare suspiciously at the pair as they get back to their feet and come after me. This can't be right. I can't have got through the group as quickly as that. I start replaying the battle, trying to put each step in order. Then the boy and woman are digging at my eyes and I have to scrap the analysis or face an embarrassing last-gasp defeat.

Falling back on my most basic defensive move, I headbutt the woman, then the boy. As they reel away from me, I follow like a hound, make a fist and start punching at their heads. Several sharp blows later, I've smashed through both skulls and pulped their brains.

Rising slowly, head spinning, I set my sights on the last three zombies. The girl with the snapped neck is spinning around, tugging at her head, trying to fix it. I slip up behind her, nudge her towards the bars of the cage, then slam her into them to finish her off.

The woman whose head I kicked is still writhing in the dirt. She's probably no longer a threat, but I limp across, raise my foot high, then bring my heel down on her skull a few times until she falls still forever.

That just leaves the headless guy. His body is stumbling around, fingers twitching as he searches for his missing head. I drag my weary carcass over to where his severed head is lying, pick it up, then hurl it with the last of my strength at the bars of the cage, where it shatters like a melon. The humans behind the cage shriek and dart out of the way of the blood and flying scraps of bone and brain. The man's body slumps.

I slump as well. I stare numbly at the corpses, then catch Vinyl's eye and give him a shaky thumbs up. 'Too easy,' I wheeze, then cover my eyes with an arm and make a hoarse, choked, wheezing sound which is something between a triumphant chuckle and a horrified sob.

FOURTEEN

The humans are cheering loudly. Some push forward and bang the bars of the cage, letting me know that they considered this first-rate entertainment. Maybe they would have viewed it differently if they'd had to crack open those skulls using their own hands.

I recall the expressions of the men I killed, the women, the children. And try driving them from my thoughts as soon as the grisly images pop into my head.

I force myself to my feet and drag myself across to where Vinyl is hanging. He stares at me with disbelief. 'If I hadn't seen it, I wouldn't have believed it,' he murmurs. 'You were like a whirlwind of death.'

'I did what I had to,' I grunt. 'They were dead already. I simply put them out of their misery.'

'I know. But one against twelve ... Damn, girl, you're the hottest thing on two legs since Bruce Lee.'

I chuckle weakly, even though I don't really want Vinyl's compliments. I'd go without compliments for the rest of my life if I could bring back even a single one of the twelve people now lying dead in the cage. I don't want to be a warrior of great repute. I simply want to be able to stop killing.

'Thanks, B,' Vinyl says softly. 'I know it can't have been easy.'

'You have no idea,' I sigh, rolling my neck, fighting the pain, trying to stay focused. I can barely stand. I don't know how I kept going during the battle. It would be nice to think I could enjoy a well-earned rest at the end of this, but I know Dan-Dan's torture table is all that awaits.

I turn creakingly and look for the despicable child-killer. He waves at me, then clasps his hands over his head and shakes them as if we'd just won a big match. My dad is close by, smiling proudly. The fool.

I raise a hand for quiet, and to my surprise everyone shuts up instantly. Maybe they think I'm going to make a victory speech.

'I won,' I call to Dan-Dan. 'Set Vinyl free, like we agreed.'

Dan-Dan squints at me. 'I don't recall us striking a deal. In fact I don't think we even discussed one.'

I start to tremble, but quickly suppress the tremors, not wanting to show any fear. 'Don't mess me about,' I growl. 'I fought the way you wanted. I killed as you wished. Let him go.'

'Yes, Daniel,' Owl Man pipes up. 'She duelled in good faith. Do the decent thing and free her friend.'

Dan-Dan blinks at Owl Man, then cocks his head at Justin and Vicky Wedge. 'What do you think?'

'We don't do deals with the undead,' Vicky grins.

'Life isn't fair,' Justin says. 'She failed to set her terms before she fought, so she can have no legal comeback.'

'Bullshit!' Josh roars, surprising me with his support. 'We make the laws here, and I say she's done enough. Let the boy go. In fact you should let her go too.'

Some of the people around the cage mutter their approval, but Justin takes the challenge to his authority in his stride.

'*You* do not make the laws here, Mr Massoglia. *We* do.' He gestures at himself, Vicky Wedge and Dan-Dan. 'We are the cement which binds the Klan with the army. If you remove us from the equation, the result will be anarchy. Who wants that?'

Nobody answers his challenge. Many look shifty and stub the ground with their toes, but nobody speaks up against him. Justin casts his gaze around, snorts with satisfaction, then addresses Dan-Dan again.

'You can decide what to do with the pair, Lord Wood, as is your right.'

Dan-Dan scratches his chin and pretends to be caught on the horns of a moral dilemma. 'Well, I don't want to be unfair to the girl,' he muses aloud.

'She fought like a lioness defending her cubs, and it would be wrong to ignore that. At the same time, let's not forget that she's a zombie. Murder is in her blood. And the boy is her accomplice.'

'This isn't looking good,' Vinyl croaks behind me as Dan-Dan sighs and rolls his eyes theatrically.

'Keep the faith,' I tell him, even though I don't have any myself. I pin my gaze on Dan-Dan, hoping against hope that he'll show some small shred of mercy, if only to keep his supporters quiet.

'Tell you what,' he finally declares, 'let's put a deal in place. The pitiful, undead wretch doesn't deserve it in my opinion, but I'm a reasonable man, and it will give her something solid to fight for.

'Three more contests,' he says to me. 'If you win all of those, your friend can walk free.'

I stare at him sickly. 'You mean I'll have to fight three more times?'

'Yes,' he beams. 'And, to keep it interesting, we'll add another four zombies to the mix each time.'

'No!' someone roars, and I realise with numb

shock that it's my dad. 'You're out of order. That's asking way too much of her.'

'Be careful,' Dan-Dan snaps, 'or I'll stick *you* in there.'

'Todd has a point, Daniel,' Owl Man says. 'If you make her fight back to back, she will surely fail. You should give her a sporting chance, time to recover between bouts, maybe a weapon if the number of opponents are increased.'

I look back at him, then at Dan-Dan. If I'm afforded a decent break each time, and a weapon . . .

Dan-Dan's smile kills the bloom of hope before it can fully form.

'*Time?*' he hoots. 'Nonsense. She's a zombie. She doesn't need to rest, and I'm wary of her breaking out if we give her a weapon. We'll stick in her next sixteen opponents right away and, if she defeats those, the next round will take place after that, and . . .' He rolls a finger around in the air. 'You get the idea.'

Dad gawps at Dan-Dan, unable to believe his ears. Me, I don't have ears any longer, so I've no problem believing him.

'B,' Vinyl says as Dan-Dan sends some Klanners off to rustle up another batch of prisoners to be infected and set against me.

'Yeah?' I mutter, not glancing back, not wanting him to catch my distraught expression.

'We're screwed, aren't we?'

'No,' I lie. 'I feel good. I reckon I can –'

'B,' he says, sternly this time. 'If you're going to lie to me, have the decency to look me in the eye.'

I turn, wincing as my bones creak and my flesh tears. I stare at Vinyl for a moment, then shake my head softly. 'I'll give it my all, but there's no way I can beat a group like that again. I'm running on fumes. I got lucky last time, but it took everything out of me. I'm sorry.'

'Nothing to apologise for,' he smiles. 'You were immense. I'm honoured that you fought on my behalf.' A sly smirk crosses his face. 'You wanna help me turn the table on these suckers, really stick it to that lunatic in the sailor suit?'

'You have a plan?' I ask incredulously.

'You know me,' he smirks. 'Always a few steps

ahead of everybody else. That's why they sent me to a school for brainiacs.'

'I can't wait to hear this one,' I wheeze sceptically.

'It's simple enough. They can only make you fight if you have an incentive. Take me out of the equation and they're scuppered.'

'Yeah, but how am I gonna do that?' I frown. 'Dan-Dan won't let you leave this cage until . . .'

I stumble to a halt. I see now what he's asking. I was never as sharp as Vinyl, but I'm no dummy either.

'Don't think about it,' Vinyl snaps before I can argue. 'You know it's the only way. Hurry up and do it before they spot the danger and separate us.'

'Vinyl . . .' I croak.

'I know,' he sighs.

He's right, of course. It won't be much of a victory, but the alternative is letting him be torn apart by a pack of undead strangers. I've watched people succumb to zombie attacks. It's dreadful, the fear they experience, the haunted look in their eyes as their skulls are cracked open, knowing what's to come, that their bodies will be violated even in death.

157

I step up next to Vinyl. He stands to attention, holding his chin high, eyes set straight ahead.

'You're sure?' I ask him.

'Yeah,' he grunts.

'Any last words?'

'See you in Heaven.'

I smother a snort. 'You really think they'd let me in?'

'I'm sure of it,' he says softly, then smiles. 'After all, you're an Angel.'

'And you're an arsehole,' I snicker.

'Takes one to know one,' Vinyl laughs. Then he steels himself. 'Do it now before I lose my nerve.'

I reach out towards him.

'Hey,' Vicky Wedge says. 'What's going on in there? Daniel, stop them! She's going to –'

But before Dan-Dan or anyone else can interfere, I grab hold of Vinyl's head and whip it savagely to one side, snapping his neck, killing him on the spot. Then I bite into his skull and rip through his brain with my fingers, making sure I finish him off completely and set him free.

FIFTEEN

'*No!*' Dan-Dan howls, his face reddening with rage. 'She can't do that! Stop her!'

'I think it's too late, Daniel,' Owl Man chuckles.

'Bring him back,' Dan-Dan shouts. 'Turn him into a zombie.'

'You need brains to become a zombie,' I sneer, flicking bits of Vinyl's grey matter in Dan-Dan's direction. 'But if you want to come in and check if I've left enough of his brain intact, be my guest.'

Dan-Dan's eyes nearly pop out of his head. He starts forward and I think he's actually going to be dumb enough to enter the cage. Then reality kicks in and he draws to a halt. Jaw trembling, he thinks for a moment, then barks at my dad. 'Smith! Go in there and see if there's any hope.'

Dad nods obediently, opens the door of the cage and enters. He hurries across, barely glancing at me, focused on Vinyl. He passes close by. I could reach out and gently scratch his cheek, or tackle him and snap his neck. But I don't. For all his flaws, as I've noted bitterly many times before, he's still my dad and I love him.

Dad stares into the hole in Vinyl's skull. Then he steps back and shakes his head.

'Damn.' Dan-Dan actually stamps his foot like a pantomime villain. 'What sort of a hellish demon did you raise? He was her best friend, yet she killed him as if he meant nothing to her.'

'It was because of her feelings for him that she removed him from your grasp,' Owl Man answers. 'You pushed her too far, Daniel. If you had given them even a glimmer of hope, she would have carried on. But they knew they were doomed. She had nothing to fight for, and the boy obviously preferred to die at a friend's hand.'

'It's easy to be wise after the fact,' Dan-Dan huffs, shooting me evils.

Dad hasn't moved. He clears his throat and addresses his foul master. 'If you want to chain me up in her dead friend's place, Lord Wood, I won't resist.'

Dan-Dan blinks, taken aback by the offer. 'Why are these cretins so ready to sacrifice themselves?' he growls.

Justin is laughing. 'You never were very good at understanding the mentality of the common folk.'

'There's nothing common about that family and their cohorts,' Dan-Dan spits. He stares at me, weighing up his options, then pulls a face. 'No, Todd, your offer is appreciated, but the game has been spoilt. Besides, I'm not sure she would fight as valiantly for you as she fought for her boyfriend.'

'I want to see more,' Vicky Wedge pouts.

'Then find your own thinking zombie to dance for you!' Dan-Dan screams. She cringes and falls silent. He looks at me again, like a petulant, overgrown child. I flick him the finger and he bares his teeth. 'You think you've got the best of me, don't you?'

'No,' I mutter. 'But I got under your skin for a minute and I spared Vinyl any more of your torment. That's enough for me. I don't care what you do to me now. Torture away to your heart's content.'

Dan-Dan sighs, the rage draining from him as swiftly as it formed. 'No. I don't have the heart for it now. You,' he nods at Rage, who has been watching with a wry smile. 'Go in there and subdue her. Kill her father first, just in case that hits her where it hurts. Then finish her off.'

'Do you want me to make it slow?' Rage asks, cracking his knuckles.

'I couldn't care less.' Dan-Dan yawns irritably and casts his gaze over his retinue of children, gathered in a cluster behind him. 'I'm going to retire with my darlings when this is over, spend a week or two shut off from the world, with only my little cherubs for company. I feel terribly tired all of a sudden. I need to recharge my batteries.'

Owl Man calls to Dan-Dan as Rage steps through the open door of the cage. 'I'll ask you again, Daniel. Don't do this. Give her to me. There is more to the girl than you ever imagined. You should stop treating her as a plaything.'

'I'm through treating her as anything,' Dan-Dan says. 'Bored now. I'll hang around until the other zombie pulps her brain, then I'll be glad to see the back of her.'

'And if she overcomes your latest foot soldier?' Owl Man asks.

'She won't,' Dan-Dan sniffs. 'She's through. This isn't a contest, just housecleaning.'

I turn to Dad, who looks far calmer than I thought he would. 'This is what you get for taking the side of creeps like Daniel Wood,' I tell him.

Dad shrugs. 'I'm sorry about Vinyl. I know you liked him. He would have been a good kid if –'

'What?' I snap. 'If he'd been white?'

Dad smiles thinly. 'It's too late for me to change my ways. I know you never saw eye to eye with me on this. If we'd had a few more years, maybe I could have convinced you, but that's the way it goes. I've no hard feelings, B. Regardless of our differences, I always loved you.'

'Yeah, well, you had a funny way of showing it,' I whisper.

'Come on,' Rage booms, taking up position in the centre of the cage. 'Let's get it on.' He beckons me forward.

'You gonna fight for me?' Dad asks.

It's my turn to shrug. 'I suppose. You're not really worth the effort, but Mum would want me to.'

'You don't have to,' he says. 'We can blow this joint together, ruin their plans the way Vinyl did.' As I stare at him uncertainly, he carefully reveals the top of the grenade which he showed me before. 'This is how I'll choose to go if that guy gets the better of you. I don't mind doing it now, with you by my side, if you've had enough.'

I gaze at the grenade, imagining the moment of explosion, one short flash, one decimating blast, then lights out. The escape I've been longing for.

But when did I ever take the easy option? I feel like

I'd be letting down the team if I rolled over now. I've defied the odds plenty of times before. Maybe Rage will slip and crack his head open, or he might spontaneously combust. Perhaps I'll find one last spark of energy and expose a weak point. Massively unlikely, but if there's a fight to be fought, I'm compelled every time to stand my ground and face it. I'm a sucker for lost causes.

'Wait a bit,' I sigh. 'They might let you live once I've been dealt with. Don't be in a rush to blow yourself up.'

I turn my back on Dad and start towards Rage.

'B,' Dad stops me and winks when I look back. 'Give 'em hell, girl.'

'I'll do my best,' I grin weakly and advance.

Rage is waiting for me, smiling wickedly, thumping his right fist into his left palm.

'I would have dreamt of this moment if I'd been able to sleep,' he says. 'I've known it was coming since we first met. No,' he corrects himself. 'Not since the very beginning but early on. There was something about you. The others were fodder but you . . . I knew we'd have it out with each other further down the line.'

'You should have killed me in the underground complex when you had the chance,' I growl.

'And miss out on all the fun times we've enjoyed?' he hoots. 'You've been a joy to spar with. I'm just sorry it has to end so soon. I was hoping to lock horns with you for years to come. As they say in those old spy films, you were a worthy adversary.'

'Will you tell me something before you kill me?' I ask.

'Depends what it is,' he smirks.

'Remember what the Board suggested when they brought us here?' I whisper. 'That Dr Oystein might have sent you in as a spy, that he told you to kill Pearse and Conall to make it look like you were on Dan-Dan's side? Any truth to that?'

Rage stares at me coldly. 'Why do you care?'

'I used to hate you,' I tell him. 'Then I grew to respect you. If you really are a heartless bastard, I'll be mad at myself for buying your act and letting myself start to trust you. But if you're secretly still on Dr

Oystein's side, it'll give me hope that this poxy crew of power-hungry maniacs can be brought down, and I won't go to Hell cursing your name.'

'I don't care about a few curses,' Rage says.

'Come on,' I urge him. 'Nobody can hear. I won't give you away. Level with me.'

I don't know why it matters. Maybe I'd grown to like Rage more than I ever acknowledged. Maybe I need to believe that goodness exists in the least likely of places, that not everyone is rotten to the core, even those who most appear to be.

Rage holds my gaze for a few solemn moments, then sighs and shakes his head. 'I must be getting soft, because I'm tempted to lie and tell you what you want to hear. But no, I'm not here on Dr Oystein's business. He didn't tell me to kill Pearse and Conall.'

I nod miserably. 'I figured as much but I had to ask.'

'But if it's any consolation,' Rage adds, 'I didn't switch sides randomly. I had a good reason for cutting my ties with the doc.'

'Care to elaborate?' I ask.

He smiles icily. 'No. All I'll say is that you should have paid more attention when your mate, Billy Burke, staggered into County Hall with all guns blazing.'

'What does Burke have to do with this?' I frown.

'He discovered the truth of the old cliché,' Rage says. *'A little knowledge is a dangerous thing.* That night when we were bringing Dan-Dan back, when I left you to go off on my own, I returned to Brick Lane, to get to the bottom of the matter. I like to know things. I found out that –'

'What are you waiting for?' Dan-Dan shouts. 'Are you trying to bore her to death?'

Rage laughs. 'My master's voice. Sorry, Becky, but my big revelation will have to wait. A pity, as it was a real killer. I wish I could have shared it with you. I think you'd have seen the bitterly funny side, like I did. Or maybe it would have driven you demented, like Burke. I'll try to tell you if you're still conscious after I've disabled you, before I rip your brain out of your head.'

'Come and get me, big guy,' I snarl and step

forward into range, ready for the final fight of my life.

A guard on one of the roofs yells a warning through a megaphone before Rage can throw the first blow. 'Zombies! Coming out of the river!'

'Zombies!' a guard on a different roof echoes.

Soon guards everywhere are bleating, 'Zombies! Hundreds of them!'

'Thousands!'

'They have us surrounded!'

'Calm down,' Justin roars as panic sets in. He grabs a megaphone from one of his people and addresses the guards on watch. 'Are the sirens working?'

There's a short delay, then the answer comes back — the sirens are functioning as normal.

'Are the zombies pressing forward past the outer ring of speakers anywhere?' Justin asks.

That's a negative. No zombie has breached the invisible, high-pitched barrier.

'Then there's nothing to worry about,' Justin says smugly. 'I don't know why the beasts have gathered, but they can't harm us. We'll deal with them later. Now let's return to more pressing business.' He turns his attention back to Rage and me.

'Wait,' a soldier yells. 'It's not just zombies. There are mutants too.'

'Where?' Justin roars, losing his composure.

'Over here. A few dozen of them.'

'Anywhere else?' Justin bellows.

The other guards start reporting that there are mutants mixed in with the zombies on all sides. Justin looks uneasy now. Everyone does.

'What's happening?' Vicky Wedge squeals.

'Shut up,' Justin snaps, turning to Owl Man. 'Zachary? Do you know what the mutants are doing here?'

Owl Man shakes his head calmly. 'I have an idea but nothing more.'

'Then share it with us,' Justin thunders.

Owl Man smiles and starts to respond, but is interrupted by a guard on one of the walls. 'The mutants are unfurling a banner. It's some sort of drawing.'

'Here too,' another calls.

'Here.'

'And here.'

'Tell me what you see,' Justin yells when the guards fall silent.

'Not much yet,' one of them answers. 'They're still unfurling it. It's big, takes several of them to handle it. Wait . . . it's coming into focus . . . it's a drawing of somebody's face.'

'Mr Dowling's, I bet,' Dan-Dan mutters nervously.

'Is it a clown?' Justin hollers.

'No,' the guard replies. 'It's a normal person. It's a . . .' He falls silent again.

'What is it?' Justin practically screams.

'It's a girl's face,' the guard shouts back at him. Then, as everyone gawps, he points a finger at me and croaks, 'It's *her*.'

SIXTEEN

Justin and Dan-Dan dash to the top of the nearest wall to check on what the soldiers have reported. A nervous hush has descended. Most of the soldiers and Klanners in the yard are ascending to view the undead threat for themselves, but they climb silently. My sense of hearing doesn't work quite so well since Dan-Dan sliced off my ears, but my nostrils are fine (he must have been saving them for the next round) and the smell of sweat is strong and sweet in the air.

Vicky Wedge and Coley remain down below, close to the cage, under orders from Justin to keep an eye on me. Josh has followed the others to the higher levels, but Owl Man has stayed behind. He's tickling Sakarias, not bothering to hide a smug little smile.

'Any idea what's going on?' Rage asks.

'No,' I reply.

'Why the hell would a pack of mutants be carrying banners with your ugly mug on them?' he presses.

'Maybe I turn them on.'

He laughs. 'Looks like I won't be killing you just yet.'

'Why not?' I sniff. 'There's no reason to let this get in the way. I'm still up for a scrap if you are.'

'And risk the wrath of Justin Bazini? Nuh-uh. I won't touch a hair on your head until I've been given the word.' Rage takes a closer look at my scalp and frowns. 'Not that there are any hairs left to touch.'

I almost ask him if I look as bad as I feel, but I know the answer, so I don't bother. Instead I ask Dad if anything like this has happened before.

'No,' he says. 'There have been plenty of attacks by individuals, and small groups of zombies so hungry or deranged that they've pushed through the pain or deafened themselves. But we've never seen mutants.'

'You don't look too worried,' I note.

He scratches the back of his neck. 'It's odd but I'm not. I'd accepted that it was my time to die. I was sure when I came in that this cage would serve as my tomb. The commotion doesn't bother me as much as it would have done earlier.'

We wait in silence until an edgy Dan-Dan returns and shouts at Coley to shackle me and take me up top. He's huffing and puffing. I think about taunting him, but decide to save it until I know for sure what's going down.

As I'm led out of the cage by a nervous Coley, arms bound behind my back, Owl Man heads off across the courtyard, clicking his tongue at Sakarias to follow.

'Where are you going?' Dan-Dan snaps.

'My laboratory,' Owl Man says.

'*Now?*' Dan-Dan is astonished.

'There are bits and pieces which I wish to gather up.'

'Why? Are you thinking of going somewhere?'

'If the eviction notice that I'm expecting is served, then yes.'

'Zachary,' Dan-Dan stops him. 'You know what's happening, don't you?'

'As I said, I have an idea.' Owl Man stares at Dan-Dan coldly. 'Last chance. Give her to me, Daniel. Place your trust in me and it will be repaid. If you ignore my offer, I won't be able to help you.'

Dan-Dan gulps, looking from Owl Man to me and back again. 'I can't,' he wheezes. 'Justin has called for her.'

'Will you take his side over mine?' Owl Man purrs.

Dan-Dan hesitates, then scowls and recovers his arrogance. 'Always,' he yaps. 'You're nothing but a meddling scientist. *We* hold the true reins of power here and you would do well to remember that.'

'Of course, my Lord,' Owl Man chuckles, bowing sarcastically. Straightening, he sets his gaze on Rage. 'I'd like to take that one with me, to help me move some of my equipment. Have you any objections?'

'No,' Dan-Dan says. 'That ugly beast doesn't

concern me in the slightest. Do what you want with him.'

I think the glowering Rage would like to raise a few objections of his own, but he goes along meekly, keeping clear of the dog, looking less cocky than he did a few minutes ago. It seems that even Rage is wary of the mysterious, unpredictable Owl Man.

Dan-Dan leads Coley and me up the towering flights of stairs to the top of the wall overlooking the area I crossed when I first came to the Power Station. He's wheezing like a thirsty dog by the time we crest the last flight. Dan-Dan's fitter than he looks, but carrying that much weight, there's only so much exercise that he can endure. Coley is also sweating but with fear.

Justin's positioned himself in the middle of the walkway, looking out over the side-buildings and the area beyond, to where the zombies and mutants are massed. The reviveds are standing stiffly, some swaying gently as the mutants move among them, blowing whistles to hold them in place, the way they've done when I've seen them at work before.

The banner features an accurate representation of my face, or at least the way I looked before Dan-Dan carved my cheeks apart and cut off my ears and shaved me bald. It's hard to judge from here, but it must be at least six or seven metres high.

The painting reminds me of Timothy Jackson, the artist I befriended, torn apart by zombies when he tried to care for a mutant baby. The style isn't similar to his work, but the subject matter is the same. Poor old Timothy loved to paint the undead. He'd have been fascinated by the drawing.

'Are you behind this?' Justin snaps as I'm brought before him.

'Hardly,' I snort.

'You didn't set it up before you came to us?'

I sneer. 'If I had that sort of pull, I'd be powerful like you mugs, but I'm just a normal, hard-working girl.'

'More than that, it seems,' Justin says.

For a long time nothing happens and we mutely observe the ranks of zombies and mutants as they stare back at us. Finally there's movement and they part to create an avenue, along which a familiar figure comes stalking.

It's been a while since I crossed paths with Mr Dowling, but he hasn't changed much. He's wearing a green pinstripe suit and a pair of red, oversized shoes with small skulls attached to the tips. A severed face hangs from either shoulder. Lengths of gut are wound round his arms. One change is that, instead of pinning ears to the legs of his trousers, he's replaced them with tongues.

His hair looks normal from here, but I know it's really lots of strands ripped from various victims and stapled into his scalp. His face is white. Two pink-coloured, V-shaped channels have been carved into his cheeks, running from beneath either eye down to just above his upper lip.

He had a human eye stuck to his nose the last time I saw him, but that's no longer there. Maybe it fell off, or he got tired of it. Long, thin fingers, the flesh sliced away in many places to reveal the veins, arteries and bones beneath. I always assumed he pruned the flesh himself, for effect, but looking down at my similarly shredded form, I wonder if maybe the clown had a run-in with someone like Dan-Dan in the past.

Even from this distance I can see his eyes twitching madly, rolling around their sockets like marbles. And his skin is rippling, as if insects are burrowing through his flesh. Which they might be — I recall when we first met, how he spat a shower of spiders over my face.

'Unbelievable,' Justin sighs. 'What the hell is he?'

'You don't know?' I ask.

'He's not one of us,' Dan-Dan says. 'We hate and fear him as much as your Dr Oystein does.'

'He's a loose cannon,' Justin says. 'He can't be reasoned with or controlled.'

Mr Dowling does a crazy dance as he passes his supporters. The mutants cheer, but the zombies don't pay much attention. They obey Mr Dowling and his mutated followers, but it's not out of a sense of loyalty or because they admire him. It's something instinctual. They'll follow any undead or semi-dead creature who shows signs of leadership.

The nightmarish clown leaps to a halt in front of his troops, sets his hands on his hips and strikes an exaggerated pose, so that we're looking at him in profile. As we stare, a mutant steps out of the crowd. It's Kinslow, the one I first met in the Imperial War Museum on a day that feels like it was several lifetimes ago.

Kinslow is packing a megaphone. He raises it and addresses the watchers on the wall. 'We'll keep this short and simple. We know you have the girl. We want her. Deliver her to us immediately or else. You get one chance to comply. This won't turn into a debate. So have a quick chat about it among yourselves and let us know what you decide.'

Justin grinds his teeth. 'Who do they think they are,' he growls, 'coming here and trying to order us around?'

'Maybe we should give her to them,' Vicky Wedge squeaks. 'She's not that important to us. Why antagonise them?'

'Vicky might be right this time,' Dan-Dan mutters.

Justin looks at him with surprise. 'Afraid, Daniel?'

'No,' Dan-Dan says stiffly. 'But we don't know what that clown is capable of. I despise this wench, but she's not worth risking everything for. If we have to let her go, so be it.'

Justin's face is practically radioactive. 'This has nothing to do with the girl,' he roars. 'This is about that maniac challenging our authority. If we give in to him now, what will he demand of us next?' Justin turns to a soldier who is gripping a small machine. 'Are the sirens active?'

The soldier checks his readings and nods. 'As strong as ever.'

'Any evidence that the mutants have found a way to interfere with the signal or strike at the speakers or the generators?'

'No,' the soldier says.

'Then to hell with them.' Justin snaps his fingers for a megaphone. Stepping forward, he calls to Kinslow. 'We don't do deals with lunatics and their undead followers. Leave now or we'll open fire on the whole stinking lot of you.'

Kinslow laughs in response. 'That's the worst move you'll ever make, Bazini. Don't say we didn't try to do this reasonably. Although, if I'm honest, it's going to be a lot more fun this way, so I'm glad you've been a stubborn fool.'

'Get me a bazooka,' Justin snarls at one of his team. 'I'm going to blow that impudent oaf's head from his shoulders.'

As the soldier jogs off, Kinslow steps back into the crush of mutants and zombies. As we watch, Mr Dowling slowly lifts his right hand over his head. He looks like a deranged flamenco dancer. There's a long pause, then he snaps his fingers and stamps his feet.

Justin laughs. 'If that's his opening salvo, this is going to be a very one-sided battle. Now where's that damn bazoo—'

'*Sir!*' the soldier who has been monitoring the strength of the sirens cries out. 'Every speaker just went dead! The signal is down everywhere!'

Justin turns a sickly pale colour. 'Get it back,' he croaks.

'We can't,' the soldier moans. 'I don't know how

they've done it, but the speakers have been physically deactivated. We'd have to go out and repair or replace every single one of them.'

As Justin stares at the soldier with growing horror, there's a rumbling noise, the sound of thousands of pairs of feet moving forward at the same time. The zombies are advancing, and there's nothing to hold them back.

'Looks like we've got visitors,' I chirp.

SEVENTEEN

Battersea Power Station is an iconic building, set by the river, just a stone's throw from the centre of London. I can understand why the Klanners chose it for their base, and why the soldiers and members of the Board were happy to move in. But they either overlooked one key weakness, or were so confident in their system of sirens that they didn't think it would matter.

The building is made of bricks. Zombies can easily dig into brick with their fingerbones. That means they can climb it.

They stream across the wasteland and launch themselves at the walls. Soldiers and Klanners fire in a frenzy, and many of their bullets strike home, but the zombies keep on coming, a swarm of them, a dozen to replace each one that is killed. It's only a matter of minutes before they'll spill over the top.

'Stand true!' Justin screams as he hurries from his spot on the wall, Vicky Wedge flapping along behind him. 'We can hold if we're brave.'

That's a load of bullshit. He just wants to buy time for himself, so that he can slip away like he did on the *Belfast*. But if the troops are aware of that, they choose to ignore it, and most remain at their posts, pumping round after round into the zombies scaling the walls.

Dan-Dan tells one of the soldiers to give him a gun and casually aims it at me. Coley yelps and ducks out of the way as Dan-Dan squeezes an eye shut and mutters, 'Time to put you out of my misery, little girl.'

'I don't think so,' Dad says, stepping up beside me with a gun of his own.

'What are you doing?' Dan-Dan snarls.

'Protecting my daughter,' Dad answers coolly.

'You were quick enough to give her to me earlier,' Dan-Dan says.

Dad shrugs. 'I had no choice then. She was doomed no matter what. This is a different situation. Leave her be, Lord Wood. You have more to worry about now.'

'Coley!' Dan-Dan barks.

'My Lord?'

'Don't just stand there like an idiot. Deal with this impudent revolutionary.'

Coley's gripping the taser that he loves so much. He's got a gun but it's in its holster. I see him think about dropping the taser and going for the gun.

'Don't,' I growl, taking a few quick steps towards him and baring my fangs.

Coley hisses and grips the taser tighter, defending himself from me.

'Coley!' Dan-Dan howls.

'I can't,' Coley wails, his eyes wide with terror behind his sunglasses. 'If I let go of this, she'll be on me before I can draw my gun.'

'That's a risk you'll have to take,' Dan-Dan snarls.

Coley gulps and shakes his head. 'I can't,' he says again, miserably this time.

Dan-Dan swears foully, then adjusts his aim and fires a bullet through the centre of a surprised Coley's forehead. The guard drops in a sudden dead heap, blood pouring from the hole between the two orbs of his sunglasses.

'I'll deal with you two later,' Dan-Dan vows as he takes off, waddling down the stairs as fast as he can.

I stare at the slain guard, wondering what his ex-partner Barnes would have made of this. Dad isn't so bothered.

'Wait there,' he says and trots across the landing to where a soldier is reloading his gun. The soldier is carrying a ring of keys on his belt. Dad asks for it. When the soldier blanks him, Dad uses the butt of his gun to club the soldier unconscious, slips off the ring and comes jogging back. I turn away from Coley, putting him from my thoughts, and let Dad unlock the handcuffs.

'Thanks,' I mutter, flexing my fingers, glad to be free again.

'What now?' Dad asks. 'Do we stay and fight?'

'No point. There are too many of them. This place will be theirs soon.' I glance at the cages in the courtyard. 'Is there anywhere we could hide the prisoners?'

I expect a contemptuous retort but Dad nods soberly. 'There are rooms in the section where you were being held. They're secure. But only from zombies. I don't think anyone ever thought to prepare for a mutant attack. They'll be able to use machinery or ammunition to break through.'

'Let's get as many to safety as we can,' I tell him. 'Then I'll hand myself over to Mr Dowling. Hopefully he'll withdraw when he has me.'

I start down the stairs and Dad is hot on my heels.

'Why is the clown interested in you?' he pants as we descend.

'I wish I knew.'

'You could try to escape rather than surrender to him.'

'Maybe. Let's see where we stand once we –'

There are screams behind us as the first of the zombies crests the wall. I pause and look back. I can't see anything above but, as I'm hesitating, I spot Dan-Dan shepherding his flock of children into his private chambers. I wince and stare down at the yard again. It's chaos, but no zombies have got in on the ground level yet, and it will be a while before they gouge their way through the troops up top.

I turn to face my dad. 'I'm gonna target Dan-Dan. Can I trust you to start freeing the prisoners and guiding them to the safe rooms?'

Dad frowns. 'What do you think I am, some kind of freedom fighter?'

'They'll be ripped apart by zombies if we leave them there,' I shout. 'Do you really want that on your conscience?'

'It wouldn't trouble me in the slightest,' Dad says and I have to smother the urge to bite him.

'Please, if not for them, do it for me,' I growl. 'You've been a lousy father. It's time to make up for some of the crap you've put me through. For once in your life, do the right thing and be a true bloody hero.'

Dad stares at me coldly, then nods abruptly. 'All right. But for you, not them. Come help me when you're done.'

'Sure thing,' I snap, taking off.

'B,' he shouts after me. 'I'm proud of you.'

'Yeah, well, make me proud of you too,' I shout back, then hurry to the door of Dan-Dan's quarters. It's locked from the inside, but even though it's a huge, heavy door, the lock is a simple latch, designed for privacy from human eyes, not to keep out a zombie.

I'm in no shape to be battering down doors, but there's nobody else who can do it for me. Steeling myself, I slam my right shoulder into the door just above where the latch is. I almost faint with the pain. If I was alive, I'm sure I'd black out, but it takes a lot to short-circuit a zombie's brain.

I slam into the door again, then a third time. Thankfully the lock snaps and the door swings open. I don't think I could have managed a fourth attempt.

I stumble into the apartment and go in search of

Dan-Dan. He's not in any of the living rooms. Nor is he in the room where I was tortured. I pause and gaze at the table where I was strapped for all those hours, cringing at the grisly memories. Then I force myself on, stopping only to pick up a looped belt which is loaded with knives. I remember this from the trolley. That's nowhere in sight, but the belt must have fallen off when it was being wheeled away.

I scour the rooms again, and this time I find a door hidden behind a silk screen. I open it and traverse a short corridor. At the end I come to a room with a balcony overlooking the courtyard. That's where I find the children.

And Dan-Dan.

The killer in the sailor's outfit is on the balcony, wringing his hands, staring at the sky as if on the lookout for God.

'Come on, come on,' he mutters. 'Where are you?'

'Hey, fat boy,' I call.

Dan-Dan whirls, aims his gun and fires. I duck out of sight.

'Stay away from me!' Dan-Dan shrieks.

'Not a hope in hell,' I chuckle. 'You're mine, sicko.'

'How are you going to take me?' he counters. 'I have a gun. If you try to rush me, I'll shoot you through the brain.'

'You'd better hope your finger doesn't shake,' I taunt him, 'because if you miss, it's goodnight, sweet Lord.'

Dan-Dan hesitates, then giggles. 'I have a better idea. If you come for me, I'll shoot a few of my darlings first. How does that sit with you?' My face darkens and he laughs at the silence. 'Let me go, Becky. There'll be a helicopter coming for me any second now. Just let me fly away and I'll leave my darlings behind. Does that sound like a fair deal?'

'It might to her,' someone replies before I can, 'but not to me.'

My head snaps round and I spot Rage lurking behind me. Sakarias is with him, the dog's fangs exposed, growling softly. I would have heard them sneaking up on me if my ears hadn't been removed, distorting my hearing. I whip out a knife and prepare to defend myself.

'Easy,' Rage soothes me. 'I'm not the enemy this

time. Owl Man sent me. He figured you'd come here and thought you might need help.'

'From you?' I sneer.

'Me and the dog,' Rage says, then calls to Dan-Dan again. 'Owl Man gave me a message to pass on. He said the Valkyries aren't flying today.'

'What the hell does that mean?' Dan-Dan shouts back.

'Well, I'm no expert,' Rage drawls, 'but I guess it means he intercepted or disabled your emergency call to the helicopter crew who were supposed to come rescue you if something like this happened.'

Dan-Dan's horrified wail is sweet music to my ears. Or would be if I had any.

'Sakarias,' Rage says, clicking his tongue. The sheepdog looks up. 'Gun.'

Sakarias barks, then darts round the corner and bounds across the room. Rage and I stick our heads out to watch. Dan-Dan yelps and starts firing, but the dog is too fast. Just before Sakarias launches itself, Dan-Dan shrieks and throws his gun to the floor, afraid that the dog will bite and infect him.

Sakarias picks up the gun and comes trotting back. 'Good boy,' Rage murmurs, patting the dog's head. He removes the gun from its mouth and steps out into the room. 'Away from there,' he snarls at the defenceless Dan-Dan.

A pale Lord Wood drags himself away from the balcony. The children stay where they are. Most are weeping, not sure what's happening, thinking they're in trouble, but some are grinning darkly, following proceedings with a ghoulish glee that their master would have approved of if they'd levelled such a look on anybody else.

'Let's not be hasty,' Dan-Dan moans. 'Remember all the promises I made, the island, power, riches.'

'They don't matter to me now,' Rage sniffs. 'You're out of the game. I don't align myself with losers.'

'Rage ... Michael ... *please.*' There are tears in Dan-Dan's eyes. He never seemed afraid of death before. I think he never believed he was in real danger until this moment. Now that the end is upon him, he's showing his true coward's colours, and it's delicious.

'This creep's mine,' I tell Rage, ready to fight to the death if he tries to rob me of the pleasure.

'I wouldn't dream of getting in your way,' Rage purrs. I grin tightly and move forward. 'However . . .'

'*What?*' I roar, turning to glare at him, ripping a knife from its holder and pointing it at his head.

Rage doesn't flinch. He simply says, 'I know you've suffered a lot and want this more than anything else. But don't you think that lot are more deserving of the honour?'

He nods at the children gathered near the balcony.

I stare at the kids, then at Rage. 'You can't be serious,' I croak.

'We're tough bastards, you and me,' Rage says softly. 'We can take any sort of torment in our stride. But they were innocent before he got his filthy paws on them. Can you imagine what it must have been like?'

'But . . . no . . . it would be wrong to make them . . .'

'I'm not talking about making them do anything,' Rage says. 'If they don't want to soil their hands, fine, you're welcome to him. But I think they're due the first blow if they care to take it.'

Rage reaches out and prises the belt from my unprotesting fingers. He removes the knives and flicks them at the floor in turn, so that they stick in it lightly, tips embedded in the oak boards, hilts and handles quivering hypnotically.

'Take them if you want,' Rage tells the wide-eyed children.

Dan-Dan's darlings gaze solemnly at the knives. Then one of them steps forward. It's Ciarán, the boy who couldn't stop singing that first day of my torture, the one who seemed afraid of the nightmares that sleep would bring. He picks up a knife then turns to face his fallen master.

Most of the other children follow suit. There aren't enough knives for all of them. Those without a weapon hook their fingers and bare their teeth.

'Please,' Dan-Dan weeps as they advance. 'Little ones . . . darlings . . . you know I love you. Be nice to Dan-Dan.'

One of the youngest girls screams and brandishes

her knife. Before she can jab it at him, I dart forward and root myself between her and Dan-Dan.

'No,' I say quietly. As the children stare at me, I look over their heads at Rage. 'Dan-Dan told me he wanted to save them. Each time he stole a child, he tried to corrupt it, to turn the boy or girl into a mirror image of himself. If we let them do this, they'll become monsters like him . . . like you and me.'

'This is a monstrous world,' Rage murmurs. 'Maybe monsters are the best equipped to deal with it.'

I shake my head. 'We can't let them do this to themselves. We can't afford Dan-Dan that final, soul-destroying victory.'

Rage thinks it over then shrugs. 'It's your call. I don't give a damn.'

I smile crookedly at the children. 'You can hold on to the knives – you'll need them if you're attacked – but go with Rage. I'll take care of Dan-Dan.'

The children look suspicious.

'It's OK,' I assure them. 'I won't let him leave here

alive. You'll never have to worry about him again. You have my word.'

'I want to watch,' the boy called Ciarán says.

'No,' I say firmly. 'You've seen enough horrors. I won't subject you to any more. Not on my watch.'

Ciarán starts to argue. Then his face crumples. With a confused moan, he throws his knife away and dashes from the room. The other children follow, Rage trailing close behind.

Dan-Dan sighs shakily with relief. He thinks he's off the hook.

'Thank heavens for common sense. Now let's talk about –'

'Sakarias!' I snap at the dog which has held its position since Rage took the gun from it. 'Rip the bastard apart.'

As Dan-Dan roars at me with rage and terror, the mutant dog hurls itself at him. Its fangs and claws flash. Flesh is shredded. Bones are snapped. Dan-Dan's head is crushed. His guts spill out and are devoured. I watch numbly, ignoring his screams and fading gurgles, making absolutely certain that the job is finished properly. I don't feel as much satisfaction as I thought I would, just a dull sense of gratitude that I don't have to worry about Dan-Dan any more.

'The fleet has sailed, sailor boy,' I whisper, throwing a mock salute his way, even though he no longer has eyes to see me with. 'Bon voyage!'

EIGHTEEN

I back out of the room, pausing only to pick up Dan-Dan's beloved sailor's hat and toss it through the window. I click my tongue and Sakarias trots along after me, panting happily.

'You done?' Rage asks as the children stare at me with wide, hopeful eyes.

'Yeah. He's dead. It's over.'

Rage nods, then addresses the children. 'Go back into that room. Stay there until I come for you later.'

'Wait,' I stop them. 'It's messy in there. Let me go clean up before –'

'No,' Rage says. 'They need to see his remains,

otherwise they won't believe that he's really dead.'

I think about that and decide Rage is right. I nod wearily and the children file through silently. Most are crying, trembling nervously, but they hold on to one another for strength.

Rage closes the door and replaces the silk screen.

'You think that will stop the zombies from finding them?' I sniff.

'Probably not,' Rage says. 'But I'm gonna stay here with the dog until it's over, to dissuade them from exploring beyond this point.'

I squint at Rage, lost for words.

'I can't make you out,' I wheeze when I finally find my tongue.

'That's the way I like it,' Rage grins.

'What you did to Pearse and Conall . . .'

His smile fades. 'I didn't want to kill them. But they were in my way. I'd had my fill of life with Dr Oystein. It was time to move on. I couldn't take them with me, so I had to drop them.'

'I hate you for that,' I spit. 'But now here you are, helping me save the kids.'

'What can I say?' he chuckles. 'I'm a complicated guy.' As I gawp at him, he makes a sighing sound. 'You can stand here like a moron, trying to figure me out, or you can go save some people from the zombies. That's what you were planning, right?'

I nod slowly. 'The prisoners.'

Rage laughs. 'Always the hero. You and the doc were cut from the same cloth. Only not quite.' He pauses and tugs at an earlobe. At first I think he's mocking me, but then I realise he's mulling something over. 'If you make it out of this hellhole, go back to Brick Lane.'

'To the Truman Brewery?' I frown.

'Yeah, where your artist friend hung out.'

'Why?'

'You might find something there that will help you understand why I'm such a cynical sod.' He puffs out his cheeks and shakes his head. 'This world is so badly screwed. I told you once that I only linked up with the doc because I wanted to go where the action was, and that was true, but like a fool I began to hope when I was with him. He almost convinced me that I should change my ways. I started to like the idea of saving society and being one of the good guys.

'But then I found confirmation that everyone who matters is rotten to the core. I'm sure there are some truly good people in the world, but those who get to decide the future ...' He sneers. 'They're more twisted than *me*, and that takes some doing.'

'What about Dr Oystein?' I challenge him.

Rage starts to say something, then shakes his head and smiles. 'I'm not gonna paint a picture for you. Go to the Brewery. Retrace your mate Burke's last steps. See where they lead you.'

Rage raises his right hand and makes a fist. After a troubled pause, I knock knuckles with him. As he starts to withdraw his hand, I uncurl my fingers and grab his fist, or as much of it as I can with my much smaller fingers.

'I *will* kill you,' I vow as he looks at me questioningly, 'for what you did to Pearse and Conall and all the others you've betrayed.'

Rage laughs. 'Someone's got to do it one day, and

I'd rather it was you than anyone else. But I won't go easily.'

'Later, Michael,' I snort.

'Later, Becky,' he chuckles, and we part, not on good terms, but with respect.

NINETEEN

I hurry down the stairs, though I can't run as fast as I could have a couple of days ago. My limbs feel like they're going to drop off. My insides are coming undone — blood is seeping through the rips in the bandages, and guts are poking through. Every time I take a step, it's like I'm bringing my feet down on crushed glass.

Still I press on. As long as there's a shred of energy in this undead body, I'll push it to the max. Pain is part of the package. I've learnt to put up with it. In a weird way, I welcome it. At least when I'm in agony,

I know this is reality, that I'm not dreaming, strapped to Dan-Dan's table in a delirious haze. If this was the work of my fevered brain, I'd have rid myself of the torment ages ago.

I hit the ground and hurry to a cage packed with prisoners. I wasn't able to save Vinyl, but I'm determined to rescue as many of his townsfolk as I can, along with the others who have been held captive here over the past few weeks and months.

The humans in the cage are screaming for help. They can see the zombies spilling down from the walls. They know their time is limited.

As I pound at the lock, I look for my dad, wondering if he kept his word or has locked himself away in a small, dark room, in the hope that he'll be overlooked in the mayhem. At first there's no sign of him and I fear the worst. But then I spot him coming out of the part of the building where I was first housed.

Dad races to my side. He's acquired another ring of keys since I last saw him, and he swiftly finds the right key for this lock. As he opens the door and waves through the prisoners, he smiles at me.

'Bet you thought I'd done a runner,' he says.

'It never crossed my mind,' I lie.

'Lord Wood?' Dad asks.

'Sorted.'

He grunts and casts his gaze at the upper levels. 'They'll be on us soon.'

'I know.'

'We won't be able to free everyone.'

'Let's just help as many as we can. There's still time. We might –'

I draw to a halt, eyes widening with shock. There are lots of manhole covers in the courtyard. They're popping open and creatures are crawling up out of the sewers. But these invaders aren't zombies or mutants.

They're *babies*.

'What the hell?' Dad cries as the unnatural infants propel themselves at any nearby soldiers and Klanners. The tiny children all look the same. They're dressed in white gowns. Their eyes have no pupils and are normally pale orbs, but now they're red, the colour they get when the babies are angry.

You'd think that babies should be easy for an adult to fend off, but that isn't the case. These hellish infants have tiny fingers, but jagged nails and long, sharp fangs. And they can move swiftly, darting about the place like ghostly eels, almost too fast for the eye to follow.

For a moment I think that the babies have come to help, that they'll only target soldiers and those in hoods. But then they start picking off the freed prisoners as they race towards the holding cells, and I see that they'll strike at anyone who moves.

'Come on,' I roar at Dad, dragging myself to the next cage.

'What are they?' he yelps, stumbling after me.

'The babies from my dreams.'

Dad gawps. 'They can't be.'

'Tell *them* that,' I huff, then rattle the lock at him. 'The key. Quick!'

Dad stares at the murderous babies, the screaming, bloodied humans, the zombies and mutants streaming down the stairs. He gulps and whispers, 'This is insane.'

'It's the way of the world,' I snap. 'Deal with it or go have a breakdown. But if you plan to bugger off, give me the keys before you leave.'

Dad scowls at me. 'Keep your knickers on. I'm doing my best.'

Turning away, Dad finds the key, unlocks the door and tells the people where to head, pointing across the courtyard.

I watch helplessly as they try to pick their way through the fighting, dodging soldiers, Klanners and babies. Not all of them make it. Some don't even try — a few set their sights on the hated members of the KKK and tackle them, trying to beat the zombies to the punch. They don't care that they're signing their own death warrants. They want payback before they die.

We manage to unlock another three cages. Then the zombies and mutants hit the scene and the carnage ratchets up a dozen notches. As the undead lay into the humans, mewling with delight as they rip open heads and dig out fresh chunks of brain, the mutants hurry to the walls and start setting explosives. They obviously plan to blast holes through them, to let in everyone on the outside. I guess they want to please all of their revived forces, even those who aren't natural climbers.

'Time we pulled back,' I tell Dad.

'You're sure?' he asks.

I nod. 'We're done here. We have to help those we've already released. With our aid, they might stand a chance. The rest . . .' I shake my head sadly.

Dad nods and we streak across the yard, the desperate screams of those we've left behind echoing after us, ringing through my head, making me wish that Dan-Dan had taken a hot iron to my ear canals and rendered me deaf.

TWENTY

I keep close to Dad, steering him clear of the worst trouble spots, shouldering a few zombies out of his way when they attack. At one point a baby darts at his legs and I pause to kick it clear. It feels wrong to kick a baby, even one as nightmarish as this, but a menace is a menace, regardless of its size.

We make the shelter of the section where the zombie-proof cells are housed just as there's a massive explosion behind us. As a cloud of dust sweeps through the courtyard, we slip into the gloom of the corridors and take stock. A lot of people have already locked themselves in, swinging the doors shut, not worrying about the fact that they can't unlock them again without help.

The freed prisoners aren't the only ones seeking the safety of the cells. Many of the Klanners have sought sanctuary too. Agitated members of the two groups clash in some places, in cells or the corridors. I leave them for the zombies to finish off, figuring you can't help those who won't help themselves. Instead I push ahead, calling to those who are desperately looking for a place to hide, leading them on.

Dad darts ahead of me, checking cells, calling out the number of people they can hold. 'Ten. Eight. Sixteen.' He pauses at one door, does a quick calculation, then shouts, 'Fifty.'

As the humans pile in and we shut the door behind them, people at the rear of the crowd start screaming.

'You deal with this lot,' I bark at Dad. 'I'll try to slow things down back there.'

'Becky,' Dad yells after me. 'What about us? We need to hole up too.'

'Do what you feel you have to,' I grunt, pushing through the panicked humans.

When I get to where the living are scrapping with the undead, I find it's the babies who have followed us. They've been tearing into the humans, but pause when they see me. I'm weary. I just want to roll over and die. But, ignoring my body's pleas, I take a stance and beckon them on, readying myself for one more round in what has come to seem like an endless battle.

The babies stare at me as the people peel away and follow Dad. Their eyes start to dim, the red glow fading to white. Then, in chorus, they speak in the high-pitched voices which I know so intimately from my dreams.

'*mummy. we love you mummy. come with us. come home.*'

'I'm not your bloody mother,' I snarl.

'*mummy,*' they screech, holding out their clammy little hands, as if they want me to take them for a walk.

I back away from the unnatural infants, shaking

my head, denying them as I did in my nightmares. I wait for their mood to switch, for them to hurl themselves at me and tear me apart, as they always did on the plane in my dreams. But they only gaze at me neutrally, arms extended, letting me go.

I limp along one corridor, then another. I find Dad and the remaining humans. He's locked another batch in and is jogging ahead, looking for the next suitable cell. 'Full,' he mutters. 'Full. Fu–' He pauses by one of the doors, staring silently through the small glass window.

The last few humans push past my motionless father, searching for their own room. Before they can find one, zombies flood into the corridor from the far end and lay into them.

'Dad!' I bellow.

He looks round, clocks what's happening, starts towards me. Then he draws to a halt. I glance over my shoulder. Mutants are standing behind me, lots of zombies mixed among them, held in place by their whistle-toting masters.

Dad smiles crookedly. 'Looks like this is it, B.'

'Wait,' I shout. 'We can cut a deal with these guys. They can –'

'Nah,' Dad stops me. 'Don't you recognise this place? That's your mum's room.' He nods at the door where he'd paused. 'It's destiny, this. I didn't wind up here by accident. I can recognise my exit scene now that I've come to it.'

Dad tosses me the ring of keys then draws the grenade out of his pocket. As I watch mutely, helplessly, he strolls to the door and opens it. I hear Mum's excited moans inside. She thinks it's feeding time.

'I'll take her with me,' Dad says softly. 'You were right. I was wrong to keep her like this. I'll go to her now and we'll be husband and wife again, if only for a few seconds.'

'You don't have to do this,' I cry. 'Just lock yourself in.'

'And stand there looking at her, listening to her, and have to deal with all that I've done?' Dad shakes his head bitterly. 'No thanks.' Then he beams at me and it's like we've stepped back a few years and he's

221

his old arrogant best. 'Don't ever forget that you came from the finest stock, Becky Smith. Your mum and me, we were the best of the best.'

'Yeah, well, you're half right,' I grin.

'Cheeky monkey,' he laughs, tipping me a wink. 'Godspeed, B. I hope it works out for you, I really do.'

'I love you, Dad,' I call after him as he steps inside and swings the door halfway shut.

'Not as much as I love you,' he shouts back. Then there's a short wait. I hear him mutter something. I catch my mum's name. A short cry of pain — I figure he's lain down on the table with her, maybe kissed her, and she's bitten him, doing what comes naturally to zombies.

Then there's an explosion. It's not as loud as the one in the yard, but it rips through my head as if it was a nuclear blast. I fall to my knees, cover the remains of my ears with my hands, and scream at the ceiling in a futile effort to drown out the dreadful, soul-crushing sound.

TWENTY
-ONE

The scream gradually dies away, but I stay slumped on my knees. I feel hollow inside. I'm a true orphan now. The last of the Smiths. Well, of my branch anyway.

Part of me wants to crawl forward to look inside the cell, but I turn my thoughts away from that. I don't need to see it. My eyes have witnessed enough horrors. I might as well spare myself the sickening sight. I'd gain nothing by looking.

A whistle blows behind me and all the zombies and mutants bow. I turn slowly, painfully, to focus on the grinning pair, Mr Dowling and Kinslow. They draw closer to me. Scores of babies glide eerily along behind them, slipping past the legs of the bowing adults, forming a circle round the three of us.

'You've come down in the world since our paths last crossed,' Kinslow says with sadistic relish.

Mr Dowling produces a bloodstained handkerchief and makes a whining noise.

Kinslow smirks. 'He says that if this can be of any help in your hour of need . . .'

I shake my head. I don't have the strength to tell him where he can stick his handkerchief.

Mr Dowling leans forward and gently tugs at one of my bandages. He looks inside and pulls a sympathetic face. Then he sticks a hand through the gap and squeezes something. I gasp with pain and he snaps back his hand, laughing like a hyena. He addresses Kinslow again.

'He apologises,' Kinslow chuckles. 'He just couldn't resist.'

I lick my dry, cracked, bloodied lips and croak, 'Kill me.'

Mr Dowling frowns. That's not what he wanted to hear. He doesn't like me this way. He wants me defiant and fiery. Too bad. This is what he's stuck with.

'*mummy*,' one of the babies squeals. There's a familiar hole in its head. I think it's the baby that Timothy rescued and nursed. '*we love you mummy.*'

'Don't they ever quit with that crap?' I groan.

'You're special to them,' Kinslow says.

'Why?' I wheeze.

He winks. 'Come with us and find out.'

'Where?' I ask.

'Home,' he says.

Mr Dowling makes more noises.

'He says it's time,' Kinslow translates. 'You've gone your own way, done your own thing, and look where it got you. He asked you to come with us before, but you refused. You can refuse again if you want. He won't force you. But he wants you to seriously consider it before you give your answer.'

Mr Dowling murmurs something and his face is solemn for once.

'He says that you belong with us,' Kinslow whispers.

I stare at the clown, his translator and their freak-ish cohorts. At the babies from my nightmares with their white eyes and vampire-like fangs. It's crazy, but for some reason I almost believe him.

'What about the humans?' I ask hoarsely.

'They mean nothing to us,' Kinslow says. 'If you want us to spare them, we will. We've killed most of those who haven't locked themselves away, but some are left, scattered throughout the building. We can call off the zombies and leave the living to regroup and free those who are housed here. This building's defences have been compromised, so they'll have to search for a fresh base. Whether they get there or not . . .' He shrugs. 'This is a dangerous city. There are no guarantees.'

'And if I don't go with you?'

He rolls his eyes. 'Obviously Mr Dowling will be upset and we'll storm out of here in a huff, leaving the zombies behind.' He taps my forehead. 'But that's not why you should come. You should come because you know Mr Dowling's right — you *do* belong with us.'

I don't know if there's any truth in that, and I'm too tired to try and work it out. All I know for sure is that, if I agree to go with them, those I fought for will be set free. Dad won't have died in vain. Rage will be able to lead the children to safety.

'All right,' I mutter. 'Take me. I'm yours.'

Mr Dowling claps with delight, then keens at the babies. They sweep forward and pick me off the floor. They lay me out flat and settle me on their shoulders. Then, as I stare at the ceiling numbly, feeling like someone who's been drugged, they scurry with me through the corridors and out into the courtyard. They come to one of the manholes, pause to readjust, then carefully lower me down to where more of their kind are waiting in the shadows, eager to manoeuvre me into place and carry me off into the darkness underground.

To be continued . . .

"A CLEVER MIX OF HORROR, FANTASY AND REALISM... GRIPPING"
THE TELEGRAPH

ZOM-B
DARREN SHAN
THE MASTER OF HORROR

"GRIPPING"
THE TELEGRAPH

ZOM-B UNDERGROUND
DARREN SHAN
THE MASTER OF HORROR

"A CLEVER MIX OF HORROR, FANTASY AND REALISM... GRIPPING"
THE TELEGRAPH

ZOM-B CITY
DARREN SHAN
THE MASTER OF HORROR

"A CLEVER MIX OF HORROR, FANTASY AND REALISM... GRIPPING"
THE TELEGRAPH

ZOM-B ANGELS
DARREN SHAN
THE MASTER OF HOR

ZOM-B
DARREN SHAN
www.zom-b.co.uk

ZOM-B BABY
DARREN SHAN
THE MASTER OF HORROR

ZOM-B GLADIATOR
DARREN SHAN
THE MASTER OF HORROR

ZOM-B MISSION
DARREN SHAN
THE MASTER OF HORROR

ZOM-B CLANS
DARREN SHAN
THE MASTER OF HORROR

ZOM-B
DARREN
SHAN
www.zom-b.co.uk